BLUES
FOR OUTLAW HEARTS
AND OLD WHORES

Massimo Carlotto

BLUES
FOR OUTLAW HEARTS
AND OLD WHORES

*Translated from the Italian
by Will Schutt*

Europa
editions

Europa Editions
214 West 29th Street
New York, N.Y. 10001
www.europaeditions.com
info@europaeditions.com

Translation by Will Schutt
Original title: *Blues per cuori fuorilegge e vecchie puttane*
Translation copyright: © 2020 by Europa Editions

Library of Congress Cataloging in Publication Data is available
ISBN 978-1-60945-569-9

Carlotto, Massimo
Blues for Outlaw Hearts and Old Whores

Book design and cover illustration by Emanuele Ragnisco
www.mekkanografici.com

Cover illustration taken from a photograph © ChristopherBernard/iStock

Prepress by Grafica Punto Print – Rome

Printed in USA

CONTENTS

To Alvaro

BLUES
FOR OUTLAW HEARTS
AND OLD WHORES

ONE

The informant looked like an ex-cop. His uniform must have been padded with mothballs and buried in his closet for years, yet the crease in his pants and the neat part dividing his thinning blond hair gave the impression he'd never risen through the ranks. I had nothing else to go on, but instinct and experience provided me all I needed to know. He had a dark mole as thick as a nickel on his right cheek. His nerve wasn't what it once was. Neither was the rest. When he talked money, his eyes lit up—brief flashes that betrayed his need to escape the tightfisted routine his pension demanded.

He said to call him Hermann, and from time to time he ran his left index finger over his lips, as if to check they were clean.

"You sure?" I asked, once more showing him the headshot of the man we were looking for.

He gave a firm nod. Convinced he was telling the truth, I handed him the envelope with 1,000 euros worth of Swiss francs. He didn't ask what we would do with the information. The answer may have spoiled his desire to spend the cash. Bouts of conscience always have to be handled with care.

Even if he had, I'd have taken pains to avoid telling him the truth. I was prepared to tell him that we had extraordinary news for the mug, that he'd become a millionaire, that an uncle who had immigrated to Brazil had named him sole heir to his fortune.

Around the clubs and underbelly of Bern we'd spread

word that we were looking for someone. The photo, ripped from a flashy magazine for affluent gourmands, showed a handsome, charming forty-five-year old with the disaffected and smug look of a winner, a look we wanted to extinguish for good.

As far as possible we'd been discreet. Bern is the city where you're likeliest to turn heads for intending to commit murder. In the end, word had reached the ears of gentle Hermann, who, so it seemed, knew the right address.

He met us at a joint that was as old as its owner and would shutter the moment she was gone. The clientele wasn't much younger. We liked the place because it was a throwback, the glasses tasted vaguely of Savon de Marseille, and every night, for a solid three hours, an Irish couple, Mairéad and Killian, played guitar and sang oldies. Folk, a little jazz, some blues. She had a boyish voice, like Bonnie Raitt. Her man, between notes, held off the ancient rage of the Northern counties. The love between them was the real reason we felt attached to the place. They'd been together for years and still knew how to laugh, kiss, hold each other's gaze. We envied those lips that sought one another out. They weren't young anymore, their faces bore the marks of a life spent gigging, but they were real. We hogged a whole table topped with glasses of Calvados, grappa, and vodka. We sat in silence and listened, toasting them with admiration and even shedding a few tears for that love that we ourselves had gone searching for, found on occasion, then lost forever, but which our outlaw hearts weren't ready to relinquish.

Hermann, the informant, slipped me a piece of paper with the address. It was typewritten, the "s" key had been used up, and you could barely make out the letters. Our man lived in the fifth district, around Spitalacker Stadium.

"What else can you tell me, Hermann?"

"Cottage. Lives with a woman," he said in halting English.

His words dispelled any lingering doubts. "When did you see them last?"

"Him the other day. Her before that."

I held out my hand. Hermann, embarrassed, hesitated before taking it. His hand was as cold as the winter that had arrived all of a sudden. He ducked out, careful to avert his gaze. Useless precaution. No one would remember an insignificant little man in the domain of those two Irish lovers.

I went back to my seat—and my drink. "Maybe it really is Giorgio Pellegrini."

Old Rossini shrugged. "Maybe. Let's get this over with."

I looked away. Max the Memory was checking the latest news on his tablet.

"We've been in Bern for over a month. If the informant's mistaken, we go back to Italy. Otherwise the cops will come around asking a lot of uncomfortable questions."

"I agree," I said. "We'll scope it out tomorrow morning."

Whenever the old owner tired of having us underfoot, we'd retreat to a quiet spot near the train station where high-end escorts came to unwind between clients. Cappuccinos, smoothies, and long sessions in the bathroom to remove the stink of their last john. Unfortunately, the language barrier didn't help improve relations, but we'd befriended a pair of thirty-something Spanish girls and a trans woman from Slovenia who spoke perfect Italian. She went by Katarina and joined our table willingly. Sometimes she'd sit there silently listening to us chatter away, and other times she'd interrupt for no other reason than to talk about hustling in Milan, her lovers, her neighbors. She kept us company for an hour that night, waiting for a high-paying john to call from the best hotel in the city. Now, for the first time, she insisted on buying us drinks. Normally we wouldn't hear of it, but when it became clear she'd take offense, we accepted.

She had a thing for Beniamino. That much was clear. Just as

it was clear that she didn't like him for a john. That was her life: screwing strangers and meeting men with whom she could dream of having something better. Katarina stroked his thin whiskers—a source of pride for the Old Gangster—and strutted off.

I'd been expecting a sad and anonymous cottage. The kind you don't bother noticing, the best kind for hiding out. Instead it was painted a bright, if elegant, color. The small garden was looked after and the hedges along the fence were planted with millimetric precision. But the white gravel drive, which led to the entrance and wrapped around the unit, lay buried in leaves that had gone to rot in the cold and rain. Hermann said he hadn't seen the woman in a few days. She must have been the one looking after the place. Unless Giorgio Pellegrini was taking care of it. But he wasn't the type to push a broom, and even if he were, he wouldn't have risked being seen in the neighborhood.

"It's deserted," huffed Beniamino, starting up the car. "Let's come back for a look when it's dark. We might have more luck."

"Maybe he's just left for a few days," added Max.

"Or else he smelled a rat," I interjected, "and he's fucked us over again."

Old Rossini engaged the gear of the subcompact with Swiss plates that had been procured for us by our landlord, an Italian who'd done a couple jobs with Beniamino twenty years back. The apartment cost as much as a suite in a luxury hotel, but it was comfortable and safe. No one would ever find us there.

We drove to a nearby neighborhood and everyone went his own way. I drank a beer and slipped inside a record shop. The owner was an old rocker with shifty eyes and a face that bespoke a steady diet of hard drugs.

"What're you looking for?" he asked in German.

"Women blues singers," I said in English, "are all I listen to right now."

He pointed to a rack, but I didn't budge. "I'm looking for something new, but I don't like combing through CDs. I'm open to suggestions."

He smiled. Without a second thought, he fished one out and handed it to me. "No way you know this one. Finnish blues."

I scanned the cover. Ina Forsman. A redhead, tattoos on her arms. "I'll take it if you let me have a listen."

"Be my guest," he shrugged, passing me a pair of battered headphones.

The guy was right. Ina had the perfect voice for songs like "Bubbly Kisses." For a while now all I'd been relishing, heart and ears, were women singers. Maybe because that was the only kind of blues that could make my desire to fall in love bearable. I thought about some of my past relationships. Just to remind myself that I hadn't always been so lonely. At a certain point I yanked off the headphones. The rocker looked at me, concerned.

I waved my hand to ensure him everything was fine, but I offered no explanation. It wasn't as if I could tell him that affairs of the heart must be swept aside when you're about to kill a man. That I wouldn't pull the trigger myself didn't matter. I'd be there and I'd feel relieved to watch Pellegrini die with my own eyes.

The last time we'd been face to face with Handsome Giorgio was in a basement, Rossini pointing a pistol at him. He bartered for his life in exchange for something more important to us, and we kept our end of the bargain. At least the Old Gangster did. I'd begged him to pull the trigger, to rid humanity of that snake, but my friend didn't listen. We'd given our word.

And yet I continued to believe that for once we could

renege on our principles. I had come to terms with that. But Beniamino hadn't.

A few minutes before 7 P.M. Old Rossini forced open the wrought iron fence. We preferred dinnertime to late night, convinced that the neighbors would be snug in their homes, distracted by the hum of the TV and the noise in the kitchen.

The door's deadbolt was no match for Beniamino's picklocks. He entered first, pistol raised. Inside, it was dark and quiet. There was nobody there. Our man least of all. A framed diploma in the hall informed us that the owner was Lotte Schlegel. My tiny electric flashlight shone on a photograph of a young woman with short black hair and a pleasant smile. How had she ended up in Pellegrini's claws, I wondered.

It was Max who noticed another photo tacked to the door of the antique solid oak closet in the bedroom. Giorgio Pellegrini smiled down at us, his arms crossed. It was the same photo we'd been handing out. Somehow he'd gotten hold of a copy, realized that sooner or later we'd find him, and split.

Max also noticed that the closet was sealed with packing tape. But it was Beniamino who took out a jackknife and cut the tape with the sharp tip.

The faint stench indicated there was a body inside. It was the owner of the house, naked, wrapped in several layers of nylon. The rope with which she'd been strangled was still wound tight around her neck. Her smile from the photograph had been replaced with a horrible grimace. We were no experts, but she must have been dead for days.

Max shuddered, his eyes fixed on the plastic cocoon shrouding the body of the latest woman to pay a high price for having met Handsome Giorgio.

Beniamino put his hand on Max's shoulder and guided him gently toward the exit.

"What now?" I whispered, disheartened, back in the car.

"Call the cops," snapped Rossini. "We've exhausted all other options."

I sighed.

Calling Inspector Giulio Campagna was never a good idea. But who was I to complain? I was the one who'd gone looking for him in a pinch. Campagna was as strange as the Hawaiian shirts he sported. He had his own theories about policing and justice. His regularly brusque, irritating tone could try the patience of a saint, but back when we'd written the final chapter in Pellegrini's criminal activity in Padua, he'd stood up for us.

Convinced that snake was nothing more than a bad memory, we'd gone back to our lives. I'd hooked up with a blues band on tour: I traveled, listened to good music, drank, and picked up a new woman every night. Breezing through life is my way of catching my breath. Then one late afternoon I got a phone call. It was Pellegrini. I should have hung up but couldn't resist finding out what he wanted. Maybe because I was on my third or fourth beer.

Pellegrini is a man of a thousand surprises, and on that occasion he didn't disappoint: he wanted to hire us to investigate the murders of his wife and mistress. Martina and Gemma. I knew them well. After their master had fled, they'd taken over management of La Nena, the restaurant Giorgio had opened and made famous.

After arguing back and forth, I declined the job, but he laughed me off: "I know you, Buratti, I've seen how you operate. You're obsessed with the truth. You won't turn this down."

His tone was too cocky. You can't trust a mug like him, even when he's telling the truth. His every move is carefully calculated. I finished my beer and went out in search of an Internet café.

From what I could glean the two women had been tortured and strangled in the restaurant cellar. The night's earnings had been found in Gemma's purse, and no one doubted that Pellegrini had been the real target.

Evidently, the two victims didn't know where he was hiding out, and their executioners ran out of patience.

That night I slept soundly, even though I couldn't put my finger on the reason for his phone call. A few hours later, I had my answer when Inspector Campagna and a few officers routed me from bed, the way cops always do, and brought me back to Padua.

At the station I made the acquaintance of Dottoressa Angela Marino. With her looks, I'd never have pegged her for a snake. I only got it when she made me listen to the conversation that I'd had the day before with Pellegrini.

There wasn't a single incriminating word, but to avoid getting life the bastard had cut a deal with this cop. It wasn't the first time. In the past he'd sold out accomplices and funneled information to cops, but now he was working a different angle for some kind of sting operation.

And we were part of the deal. If we didn't join her team, we'd wind up in jail on some trumped-up charge or other. We were hardened criminals, after all; only a long sentence was fit punishment for us.

Dottoressa Marino was persuasive. She threw Max's medical records in my face. "In his condition, he won't last more than four or five years in jail."

I hung my head. Which is to say, I pretended to give in.

My friends and I examined every possible angle, but the best solution was to uproot the problem by eliminating Giorgio Pellegrini, who had gotten us mixed up in that business just to get even. We disappeared from the scene and went after him, but he had evaded us three times. Now we were flirting with ideas and alternatives. And there was no question we needed more time. Even if we still didn't know the details, it was clear this operation was too dirty to let witnesses walk—or live. Dottoressa Marino never had the slightest intention of keeping her word. We could run or hide out in some quiet spot on the Dalmatian Coast or Lebanon, where Rossini had friends he could count on. But that, we decided, would be our emergency option. The whole business was a sick joke, an injustice we couldn't stomach. If that cop in league with Pellegrini was planning on playing us for suckers, she was sorely mistaken.

We weren't about to barter away our dignity. Not for the world. "We'll go for broke," said the Old Gangster. In seventies-era gang-speak that meant risking it all: freedom, life.

"Call him," insisted Rossini.
I fished in the pocket of my old flight jacket for my phone.

Two days later it was sunup, and I was sitting down at a little café on the outskirts of Padua, on the ground floor of a gray building bristled with antennas. At that hour, they served frozen pastries, weak coffee, dry milk that was reconstituted as soon as it crossed the Austrian border. The upshot was that it was a discreet place to meet people I'd otherwise never be caught dead with. The owner was an Albanian woman who had mastered the art of minding her own business. She'd arrived at the port of Brindisi with the first wave of boat people in '91, had busted her ass doing jobs that Italians no longer wanted to do, and had tucked away enough money to buy the place. The clientele was largely composed of retirees and homemakers, all tranquil types.

I ordered a pear juice and glanced disinterestedly at the day's news. Some priests had gotten embroiled in a sex scandal, and the story had made national TV. Parishioners, porn, sex toys, and a "boss" charged with promoting prostitution.

The press was trying to paint a morally grim picture of the affair, but the city was having a laugh. Jokes and rumors abounded, in part because the religious leaders were known and beloved for their pastoral care, and a fuck here or there never hurt anybody. It was nothing new under the Veneto sky. I once knew an old priest who described celibacy as a punishment he'd chosen. He was made of finer stuff, called bread "bread" and wine "wine," and believed it was his mission to prevent old convicts from returning to jail. When he died, I took it hard.

Inspector Giulio Campagna arrived ten minutes late. He had on a hooded parka with mangy fur lining that looked like the genuine article. He sensed my interest.

"Brush wolf," he said, pointing at it with his glove.

"You mean dog," I said curtly.

"Exactly," he said, adjusting his velvet nut-brown blazer, which hid his sidearm. "They used to sell sewer rat and call it *rat musqué*."

I shuddered to recall the bright collars and cuffs of women's overcoats. After that, nutria became the fashion. Their numbers skyrocketed after the breeding farms closed, and the provinces in Veneto waited ten years to take remedial action and institute courses for specialized hunters.

"You shaved your moustache," observed the inspector. "Lose a bet?"

"No," I answered laconically. A woman had told me it wasn't a good look, said so while slowly riding me during a romp that had, at least at first, promised to be memorable. I decided to avoid other less than stimulating moments by taking a scissors and razor to it.

The inspector looked askance at the display of baked goods. "They buy these limp-dick pastries for twenty cents and charge a euro for them."

"A euro thirty," corrected the owner.

"And don't get me started on the palm oil," he went on, raising his voice.

"Don't," I said under my breath. Campagna loved preambles. He involved other people in idle talk and didn't get around to the point until it suited him.

He stared at me a second then ordered coffee. "Sleep well?"

I lost my patience. "What the fuck kind of sting operation are we mixed up in? Please explain to me what that piece-of-shit Pellegrini is up to. He murdered a woman in Bern and now—surprise, surprise—he's vanished into thin air."

Campagna absorbed the news while pouring a whole packet of brown sugar in his cup. "I know as much as you, Buratti. They don't tell me anything. All they give me are orders I can't make sense of."

"Set up a meeting with the witch," I said, fed up. "And not at the station like last time."

"You sure that's a good idea?" he asked, checking to see that his spoon was clean. "That woman wants to fuck you over. She's making you do the dirty work and after that she'll flush you down the can."

"I have you to thank. You're the one who delivered me into the hands of that snake."

"Let me reiterate: I'm the low man on the totem pole. I do the bidding of anybody who counts for something."

"I still get the impression that she'll fuck you over too. It's not like you're her idea of a model cop."

"As long as I stay on the sidelines, I'm not running any risks."

"Bullshit. Not even you buy that."

He drank his coffee, scraped the bottom of the cup for sugar, and sucked on it pensively. "Meeting you turned out to be a real pain in my ass."

"You and your stunts torched your career long before me."

"It's a tough métier," he remarked grimly.

"I can only imagine."

"Because you're a bum. I should've thrown you in jail the minute I laid eyes on you."

I sighed. Once again the curtain fell on our little act. The inspector stood up and walked outside to place a call.

"Marino will meet you here this time tomorrow morning," he said when he came back in. Then he turned to the barista. "He's buying," he said, and left without saying goodbye.

Clearly Campagna wasn't happy about being mixed up with Dottoressa Angela Marino. Neither was I, obviously, but after Bern my chances of getting out of that situation unscathed had gone up in smoke, and now we had to fall in line with that spiteful, dangerous official from the Ministry of the Interior.

The cold hit me as soon as I set foot outside the café. I reached my car, wishing I had a parka like Campagna's. My old aviator jacket was totally inadequate, but luckily the heating in the Škoda Felicia, a car built for the colder climes of Eastern Europe, provided quick comfort. I turned on the stereo, which was more valuable than the car itself, and listened to Beth Hart croon "Baddest Blues." As usual, I had a hard time finding a parking spot around Corso Milano, where I shared an apartment with Max and, more and more frequently, Beniamino.

During sales season, Paduans stormed the stores like barbarians and clogged the parking lots downtown. When Padua fell prey to shopping euphoria, the bars filled up with people eager to show off their purchases, as if they were trophies. According to a recent study of people's emotional wellbeing, if you were to judge by emoticons, Padua was the saddest city in Italy. I believed it. Padua was beautiful, comfy as an old slipper, but in the last few years it had lost the bite that had once made it interesting.

"Padua's dying," sang Massima Tackenza, drowning in laws and a mindless urge toward order and cleanliness. The mayor didn't appreciate the sentiment, so DIGOS paid a visit to the fledgling rap group's home to have a little chat about free speech. The mayor had bought a gun and was prepared to shoot any robber with the dumb idea of burgling his residence. His bunk about reasonable force had garnered him votes, but the majority split down the middle, and for months an interim administrator had been governing Padua in the lead up to new elections.

Old Rossini, dressed to the nines, was reading the paper in an armchair in the living room.

"Campagna was no help," I told him. "I have a meeting with Marino tomorrow morning."

"I don't envy you," he said flatly. Then he put a finger to his ear. "You hear that annoying hum?"

I pricked up my ears. "Yeah, what is it?"

"The Fat Man has gotten it into his head to shed a couple pounds."

I found Max in his room, bundled in a brand new tracksuit. He'd laced up a pair of sneakers and was pedaling a stationary bike. I pretended to ignore the damp sheen covering his purple face.

"Keep your comments to yourself," he warned, short of breath.

"All right."

"If I have to go to jail, I want to be in shape."

"That's not happening."

The Fat Man looked down at his handlebars and pedaled faster.

I returned to the living room. "I hate to see him like that," I mumbled.

"He hasn't gotten over the Switzerland debacle."

That makes two of us, I thought, opening a fresh pack of cigarettes.

Max reappeared a half hour later wearing a sponge robe and cradling a fruit-and-veggie smoothie. He took the first sip like a kid being spoon-fed cod liver oil.

Rossini and I looked at each other and burst out laughing.

"How about a quick drink in the square then fish at Punta Sabioni," said Beniamino.

A look of sheer relief materialized on Max's face. "I'll go get changed."

The following morning I woke up early. After a smoke and coffee I calmly prepared my shaving cream. I needed to collect my thoughts one last time before meeting Dottoressa Marino.

It was snowing in Central and Southern Italy, and under the snow the earth was rumbling. As usual, an emergency brought out the best and worst of Italy. Fortunately the sun shone on Padua, despite the freezing temperatures. On the street I stopped into a store advertising unbeatable discounts to buy something heavier than my old jacket.

"Eskimos are back in style," confided the young clerk, as if she were sharing a secret. After sizing me up and tallying my age, she figured I was a remnant of the counterculture era.

I shook my head. I wasn't all that nostalgic. I eyeballed a simple blue parka with particularly thick lining. "I'll take that one," I said, and headed for the register.

I parked a block from the café. On my way over I passed a black sedan, fresh from the car wash. The man in the driver's seat was talking on his cell phone. He was Marino's driver, clearly. I'd find the others waiting for me in the warmth of the café.

The moment I walked in, the owner nodded toward a table in the back where the Dottoressa was sitting with Inspector Campagna and another cop, younger, who stood up and walked over to me. Wholesome-looking, except for his weasely eyes.

"You know the drill," he whispered in his thick Calabrian accent.

I raised my arms and spread my legs.

"Don't be cute," grumbled the agent, discreetly patting my sides. "No need to put on a show."

"Everybody in the neighborhood's already pegged you for cops."

Angela Marino sighed. "Leave him be, Sergeant Marmorato. Buratti doesn't pack a firearm in public. He doesn't have the balls."

She kept her eyes on me as I sat down. "Unlike Beniamino Rossini, who wears a bracelet for every man he's killed," she went on. "It'll never be too late to lock *him* up for life."

She had a pleasant voice, which made it all the more difficult to swallow her bullshit. I looked at Campagna, who was inconspicuously shaking his head, warning me not to react. I didn't intend to, not in the slightest. It was my second time meeting that hyena, and I knew she was doing everything in her power to provoke me in order to remind me who was in charge.

Once again, she wore her hair in a ponytail. Maybe she wore her hair that way for work, or maybe she wore her hair that way all the time. Two gold aquamarine earrings dangled from her ears.

She took a sip of water. "Nice of you to show up. We were beginning to run out of patience," she said. "I've earmarked three kilos of coke for you and your friends. For me to plant where I want, when I want. You know how many years you get for that? At least fifteen with my recommendation."

"We were looking for Pellegrini," I interrupted.

"I know. He told me. He thinks your objective is to eliminate him."

Well look at that, I thought, pretty Angela has a direct line to Handsome Giorgio.

I feigned indignation. "Pellegrini's wrong. All we want is to find out who could have it out for him so bad as to murder Martina and Gemma so brutally. Because there's a long list of people who have a score to settle with the guy you're protecting."

"Bullshit. You wanted to eliminate him and slink off."

I tried changing the subject. "Did Pellegrini inform you he killed Lotte Schlegel, his hostess in Bern?"

"Giorgio had nothing to do with that. It was probably the people who took out the wife and friend."

"It was him all right."

"Maybe it was you," she shot back.

I put up my arms. "What? Threatening to throw us in jail for trafficking isn't enough for you?"

The woman smiled. "I can top that."

I pretended to surrender. "What do we have to do?"

"Investigate the death of Martina and Gemma."

"Why us? Isn't that Homicide's job?"

"With your connections, I'm sure you and your friends have a better shot at uncovering the killers."

What she'd said was half true. I pressed on. "You didn't answer my first question."

"I don't have to."

The cop stood up, and Marmorato mimicked her. "From now on we won't tolerate anymore funny stuff," she said. There was venom in her voice. "Inspector Campagna will provide you with the pertinent information." She began walking away but turned around after a few steps. "I tapped my people at Interpol to get a clearer picture of your criminal contacts in Slovenia and Croatia. The local authorities cooperated. In the future, it won't be so easy to rely on your cohorts and hideouts," she added smugly. "Running isn't a viable option anymore, Buratti. You should think about turning on Rossini, once the case is closed, in exchange for immunity. For you and that derelict Max the Memory."

"Three kilos of coke are more than enough to get what you want. You don't need me."

"You're capable of nailing Rossini for every bracelet on his wrist."

"You're wrong. I'd never do that."

"Oh, sure," she replied. "You all act tough at first. But when you're facing life in jail, you'll turn on anybody."

"That's your goal is it, nail Rossini?"

"Not my main goal, obviously. But why not take advantage of the situation? Giorgio testifies to the few murders he witnessed, and you testify to the rest."

Suddenly I got it. "Sending Beniamino to jail is Pellegrini's idea, am I right?"

"He put it out there during negotiations. Involving you gives us the added opportunity to shut your gang down for good."

"We're not a gang," I answered, indignant.

"An opinion that'll definitely pique the interest of the High Court," she trilled, exchanging a playful look with Sergeant Marmorato.

"There's one thing I don't get, Dottoressa."

"Make it quick. I'm busy."

"You're presuming we'll accept being blackmailed for some bogus crime. I mean, in the end you'll do everything in your power to screw us over no matter what. Tell me, what's in it for us?"

"Wake up, Buratti. This is a contest to see who's most willing to peddle his ass," she snapped, fed up, as if she was talking to an idiot. "Prove you're willing to sacrifice everything in the name of justice and there's a chance you can save yourself."

She turned heel, and Marmorato followed. The Dottoressa had made herself clear.

I snatched Campagna's wrist. "What, none of your usual repartee to lighten the mood while that bitch measures our coffins?" I asked. I was livid.

The inspector wriggled free. He'd gone pale. "Don't make hay, Buratti."

"You were fucking played," I seethed. "Slithering around to please her won't help you: you're one of the scapegoats and fall guys too."

"You're forgetting we're both cops."

"Is that right? Too bad you count for less than zero to Angela Marino. She despises you, and she'll torch your career as soon as you're no use to her."

"Keep dreaming," he said, standing up. He took a disk out of his jacket pocket. "It's the copy of the double-homicide report, updated yesterday."

"You really think she'll let you testify in court that she ordered you to deliver a homicide report to me?"

"Maybe I'll play her game," he spat. "Maybe I don't know what the fuck to do. Not one of my colleagues will lift a finger to defend me against that bitch."

I shot to my feet and he backed up. "Think, Campagna. If you're the last cop she'd want to work with, why did she come to you?"

"Because she knows I covered for you when you forced Pellegrini out of Padua."

I threw up my arms, exasperated. "And what are you going to do to avoid military prison?"

"I don't know, Buratti. Maybe nothing. After all, I committed a crime."

"Cut the bullshit. You took the only shot you had at getting justice."

He sighed. "You and your partners are criminals. You've got absolutely nothing to do with justice."

"Neither does Dottoressa Marino," I replied.

"She's different. She was born and raised on a planet of special ops at the ministry. She doesn't think like a beat cop."

"That's exactly why we're the only ones you can count on."

"What are you talking about?"

I spelled it out for him. "We should team up, Campagna. It's the one chance we've got of walking away from this."

He stared at me a long time then silently withdrew.

"Think about it!" I said loudly. Everyone but him turned around.

I walked over to the register. First time in my life I was stuck paying for three cops.

The owner waved my money away.

"What's up?"

"It's O.K."

"I insist."

"In Albania I used to watch Italian television in secret," she began. "It was forbidden. But every night, when state TV stopped transmitting, I would tune in to Italian TV. I would watch till morning, because there was something magical about it that I couldn't put my finger on. When I arrived in Italy, I realized it was the light. Our lights were always weak and sick-looking. They never lasted long. Staring at a light bulb broke your heart. To read you had to use an oil lamp or candles. My first night in Brindisi I swore to myself I would never give up that light. I've always been careful to keep out of trouble. Italian trouble, Albanian trouble. Understand?"

I nodded. "I apologize. I won't come back."

I exited and lit a cigarette. The taste of tobacco mingled with the stink of the trash burner in the distance. The air in Padua is filled with fine dust that only rain can get rid of, but there hadn't been a drop for weeks.

I half turned to see the woman from the bar. She'd stepped out from behind the counter to help an old woman into her coat. She could have told me to get lost. Instead she'd chosen to confide something intimate to me to help me understand the importance of what she had and what I had almost jeopardized.

I felt guilty. I stopped a man with white hair protruding

from an old flat cap as he was entering, the paper tucked under his arm. He must've been on his way for a coffee or a glass of white wine. He'd stick around all morning, reading the news, offering his own running commentary.

He was suspicious, and my smile didn't assuage his suspicions. I took two fifties from my wallet and asked him to give them to the owner.

"Why don't you give them to her yourself?"

"It's an old debt. I'm too embarrassed."

He put out his hand and took the money. He had two wedding bands on his ring finger.

"Thanks," I mumbled.

I had nothing to share with my friends but bad news, so I took my time delivering it. I drove through Padua listening to Gina Sicilia's "Allow Me to Confess" and holed up in an osteria, one of the last places left where people still played cards. I lost at *scopa*, lost at *briscola*, offered everybody a round, gorged on meatballs and boiled eggs to avoid stomach cramps from the cheap wine, and got my fill of gossip and filthy jokes.

"Know what I think," remarked Beniamino, imperturbable, a few hours later, after I'd finished replaying my conversation with Angela Marino word for word. "Even if they torched our chances of hiding out with my old associates in what used to be Yugoslavia, we could always count on the guys who stayed in Beirut. But I don't have the slightest intention of running. As far as I'm concerned, the plan doesn't change."

I turned to Max. The Fat Man had been listening silently, chain-smoking.

"I can't stand the idea of an official from Interior threatening to throw me in jail regardless of my actual guilt," he said, choosing his words carefully. "Moreover, using my health to raise the specter of incarceration is frankly unacceptable. And the knowledge that her crusade is fueled by someone as deplorable as Giorgio Pellegrini and his desire for vengeance drives me mad. But that's not all. I spent a large part of my life hoping to see a happy multitude achieve their dreams. Instead I find myself surrounded by legions of individuals who are dead inside, who are resigned to being robbed of their lives."

"So?" Old Rossini prodded.

"So, in a world as cruel as this, you have to survive. Whatever the cost," he replied. "It's a question of dignity."

TWO

Old Rossini departed for Punta Sabbioni. He couldn't stomach hearing the details of Martina and Gemma's murder. Ever since losing Sylvie he had changed; violence against women had made him fragile.

The CD that Max the Memory stuck in the computer was a commodity of the digital age. Once upon a time we'd have had to flip through a file as thick as my hand, stuffed with arrest reports and photocopies of faint images. Now all you needed to do was scroll down and you had the results of the investigation as good as the originals.

First we watched the Forensics video taken at the scene of the crime, La Nena's cellar.

The camera zoomed in on the neat wood racks lined with bottles of wine and liqueurs, then fell uncompassionately on the victims' naked bodies. Their hands and feet were bound with strips of nylon that had cut into their flesh. That's how they work: the more you move, the tighter their grip. To judge by the women's disfigured bodies, the torture must have been unbearable. That was child's play compared to the mess that the piano wire had made of their necks. A sophisticated weapon beloved by hit men of a certain standing. The murderer had pulled it taut till it severed the artery. Though Gemma had already died of hypoxia, her blood, pumping from her terrified heart, had come gushing out, as evidenced by the hematic trail.

Homicide detectives had proof that there was more than

one killer. They'd come across bloody footprints from three sets of shoes, different in shape and size. Eight, ten and a half, and thirteen. Details useful in a criminal court, but for the time being they merely attested to the investigators' scrupulousness.

The scene was straight out of Grand Guignol. The killers had wanted to send a clear message, and it couldn't *not* have been addressed to Giorgio Pellegrini.

"There was at least one other man on lookout," concluded the Fat Man.

"And another in a getaway car, ready to bolt at the first sign of trouble," I added. "The restaurant is in a pedestrian zone, the first street they could have parked on was less than a block away. A thirty, forty second run with cops on their heels."

The investigators had drawn the same conclusion, and thanks to the camera of a well-known jeweler, a car had been identified parked at the entrance of a building at the exact time the killers were in the restaurant. Inside, a man, the top half of his face deliberately shielded by a Dodgers cap. He'd been forced to move by a resident who wanted to open the door to her building. The woman hadn't noticed anything unusual.

The quality of the forgery was proof that the car and driver were connected to the crime. The car was in fact a perfect replica of a vehicle that already existed. The model, color, and plates matched a Korean Berlina belonging to an unsuspecting radiologist from Milan.

"Why go to all that trouble?" wondered Max.

"Standard procedure," I said. "They always follow the same steps, they never improvise."

A deputy commissioner had profiled the perpetrators: "Based on the intelligence we've gathered, we believe these were foreign criminals with military training who belong to a highly sophisticated multitiered organization, probably mafia related."

It was in fact the absence of identifying clues that led them to believe the culprits were soldiers operating within a robust organization. They'd moved like ghosts. The dense network of cameras surveilling the city center—worthy of Orwell's worst nightmare—hadn't caught a trace of the suspects. The killers must have sent a scout to stake out a way to arrive at the restaurant without being caught on tape.

Investigators watched footage from banks and retailers, besides their own and the footage belonging to local police, dating back a week prior to the crime. Nothing.

Questioning the staff revealed that, like Pellegrini before them, the two women only stayed at the restaurant after closing time on Wednesdays, when they'd spend a few hours taking wine inventory. They'd always done good business and had chosen the middle of the week to avoid running out over the weekend.

Their assailants were aware of this little detail, which enabled them to bring the women down to the cellar knowing that they had the time and quiet they needed to act without being disturbed.

Martina and Gemma had been spied on. Yet the waiters hadn't noticed anyone who could have let the suspects in. Their accounts were all the same: they had nothing to report, there was always a lot of work to do, and their only concern was serving their customers' needs.

Their alibis were questioned thoroughly shortly after the bodies had been discovered. Investigators initially suspect people "close" to the victims, after which, absent a lead, they widen the scope of their investigation.

The clients were left alone. None was called in to testify. La Nena was, in every respect, "well patronized." Politicians, entrepreneurs, investors, loan sharks, economic representatives for the mob—everybody did business at their tables. That wasn't exclusive to Pellegrini's restaurant. As every wiretapping record proves, in Italy shady business gets done in style, over lunch and dinner. Clinking glasses is synonymous with clinching a deal.

So as not to cause unnecessary trouble or embarrassment, the police solicited information from a former colleague at the Guardia di Finanza who had left his unit to pursue a career as a real estate broker. The man, a regular at the restaurant, assured them the patrons would lead them astray.

But the investigators already knew that. Clearly, Padua wasn't the place to search for the culprits.

The informants hadn't been helpful either. Reading the various reports managed to break the somber mood. Even if their names weren't printed, they were easily recognizable, and now we had a list of every snitch in the city. In truth we'd already had a good idea about who they were. The one surprise was a guy who sold secure phones. He'd been a supplier of ours up until a couple years ago, when we dropped him because he got too expensive. We'd known him for a while and occasionally had a meal together. He was a nice guy with a fatal flaw: He was obsessed with go-kart racing. Once he got started on the subject, you had to clear out. When he raised his price, we took offense and told him to get lost. But we'd been wrong. He'd actually been doing us a favor.

"He didn't want to sell us out to the cops," I said, "that's why he found an excuse to keep us away."

"That explains a whole string of arrests among the local coke and heroine dealers," said the Fat Man. "They blabbed away thinking their phones weren't tapped, and the whole time Narcotics had their numbers."

I shrugged. "I don't give a damn about those scumbags."

We wouldn't circulate the information. There wasn't a single upstanding outlaw left who deserved that kind of courtesy.

The autopsy was required reading; we didn't want to overlook any important details. But all it revealed was how cruelly the two victims had been tortured.

We watched footage from the search and seizure of the house where they lived, the same place they had once lived with Giorgio Pellegrini. His presence there bordered on obsession. The whole place was walled with framed photographs, objects belonging to him displayed like artwork. The most ostentatious example of the power he wielded over his wife and mistress was a white room furnished with a spin bike and a sang-de-boeuf leather armchair. The women painted their nails the same color. It wasn't hard to imagine Handsome Giorgio sprawled out, relishing the sight of one of his women grinding away at the pedals.

In the closets, his clothes and shoes were kept in perfect order. Evidently, Martina and Gemma secretly held out hope that their master would reclaim his throne and bend them to his will. Even were he able, I thought, he'd never return. His cover had been blown, and Pellegrini didn't operate without a good front.

Several hours later the Fat Man's desk was littered with empties, an ashtray full of butts, and the rubbery remains of takeout pizza. It was my fault. The Fat Man had wanted to cook, but to me that seemed a waste of time.

I opened the window to air the room. "The cops did a stellar job, followed every possible lead," I remarked. "That is, every lead they could while still respecting standard homicide procedure. That's why Marino gave us the file."

"I don't follow. Go on."

"She wanted to make clear to us the limits of their investigation. To identify professional killers of that ilk you have to look for information in criminal circles, circles the police don't have access to."

"Because they don't have spies or moles."

"Exactly. The ladycop is banking on our know-how," I said. "Those guys are after Pellegrini, and Marino wants them out of the picture because Handsome Giorgio is working undercover on who knows what operation. Nothing should distract him from his main objective."

"We tried to kill him too," said Max, frowning at the memory of our failure.

"Fortunately the witch doesn't believe we can pull it off. She has too much contempt for us to consider us a threat to her man."

"Must be something big. I can't believe the lengths the police have gone to keep the press at bay," said the Fat Man. "Two women murdered like that are honeypots for the media. But they've been led astray by fake news. Journalists found the case so uninteresting, it didn't even make the local blotter."

I suddenly understood what my friend was driving at. "No leaks!" I blurted. "There wasn't the usual, inevitable news leak."

"The commerce of reports and juicy details. From politics to small-town crime, there's never any shortage of indiscretion. Yet nothing's gotten out."

"Marino must have terrified the station and the DA's office. Or maybe a government heavy contacted the high-ups at the newspapers and television stations."

Max nodded. "The story doesn't exist. That's why they have to ensure our silence at all costs."

A shiver ran down my neck to the bottom of my spine. Fear. "At least we know when they'll give us the slip."

We stared at each other and smoked. There was nothing left to say.

"Where do we begin?" I asked.

"La Nena," Max answered without hesitating. "The killers moved confidently both outside and inside the restaurant. They could count on a scout who knew what was what, so there's no doubt he went there more than once. Pellegrini taught the staff to be discreet, and they didn't make an exception with the police, but I'm sure they'll be of help."

The Fat Man was right. After all, that place was Pellegrini's acknowledged domain. Behind the facade of a high-end wine bar and restaurant operated a hardened criminal.

It was also the venue of choice of Sante Brianese, Pellegrini's old attorney, who'd risen through the ranks, from the courtroom to the Regional presidency and eventually to Parliament, only to be convicted on several charges at the end of his career. Graft and criminal conspiracy related to the so-called major infrastructure schemes. Word among the crooks in Veneto was that Brianese and Pellegrini had been in bed together for some time. It appears Giorgio used to procure party girls for the politician and his business associates, and that in exchange the lawyer tipped him off about where to invest his money. Just rumors. But I was inclined to believe them: two people that crooked were bound to conspire together.

We re-read the statements of the two chefs, the three assistant chefs, the dishwasher, and all seven waiters. Among them the name Giampaolo Zorzi leapt out at us. He didn't have a prominent position, but everyone said he was the closest to Pellegrini and therefore also to the "ladies," as the wife and mistress were called. He was the first one hired and still held the same job. Modest pay raises over the years, no career ambitions. Self-effacing, always present. The classic right-hand man. Pellegrini had probably met him before taking over the restaurant, though they had not met in jail; the man's record was immaculate.

I called Rossini. He picked up on the second ring. Despite the time, he was on the jetty outside his house, smoking in the fog.

"You could cut it with a knife tonight," he said.

"Can you be here tomorrow morning?"

"Nine o'clock. I'll bring pastries."

Max shook his head, appalled. "Not before ten. I'm bushed."

"O.K.," chuckled Beniamino, hearing the Fat Man. "But I'll be there empty-handed. They're no good after nine."

"Give me a break."

"The bakery has its rules," he answered flatly, "just like everything else in this world."

Old Rossini was in a lousy mood and ready to carry on aimlessly. It was happening with greater regularity every time he returned to that pretty house by the sea. It was full of memories, the most trifling of which tore him from bed and drove him to spend the small hours of the night torturing himself.

I hung up and sent a text to Campagna asking for more information about the waiter. He answered immediately. We'd talk the next day over breakfast.

I left Max splayed on the divan watching the nightly news and retreated to my room. My mind was assaulted by images of pain and death, and I detoxed on Danielle Nicole and her rock-inflected Kansas City blues. I drank top-shelf Calvados to help me sleep.

For a change, the inspector and I met downtown in the back of a café off the square. Once upon a time the place had been a coffee shop, and it still fronted like one too, grinding franchise beans.

The owner owed the inspector a string of favors for liberating her from a loan shark boyfriend and smoothing things over with the bank. Campagna was a good man, no question about it, but he was also a tortured, bizarre, depressed cop, a loose cannon that we couldn't, unfortunately, do without.

The cop was scanning the street, his back against a barred window.

"Starting today I'm at your service," he said, not turning around.

"Sorry?"

"They've relieved me of all my duties," he explained faintly, "and tasked me with ensuring your 'mission' is a success. Obviously they refuse to put a single word of that in writing."

"So, when the time comes to make a clean sweep, they can say you were working with us."

Campagna changed the subject. "My only regret is a case I was losing sleep over. We found out that the 'Ndrangheta has been taking over failing companies, pretending to save them, then forcing them to buy a mountain of merchandise that gets diverted elsewhere."

"So the suckers who trusted them are drowning in a sea of shit, right?"

"They defrauded 47 people. Families crushed by debt, good people desperate, knowing they'll never recover." I'd never heard him this bitter. "I busted my ass trying to nail the bastards that ruined them, and just when we're about to issue arrest warrants, they have the nerve to sidetrack me so that I can babysit three washed-up crooks."

By "crooks" he meant us, obviously. Campagna continued to dispense with common courtesy and misread the situation. Or else it was a put-on. In any case, he clearly remained far from the idea of forming an alliance to save himself.

"What did you find out about Giampaolo Zorzi?" I asked.

He finally deigned to turn and look at me.

"His older brother Marco was Giorgio Pellegrini's cellmate in San Vittore," he replied. "We can assume he was the one to recommend him for the waiter job. His loyalty was guaranteed."

"Not like he went on to a great career."

"Depends on what you mean. Maybe he's clever, maybe playing the faithful servant made him rich."

A young waitress arrived with breakfast. She was nervous and kept her eyes on the floor. Our silence made the situation worse, and she practically ran away after setting the tray on the table. The inspector extended his arm. "I arrested her when I was working Narcotics. Freaks out when she sees me."

"Makes me wonder how you treated her."

"Badly, Buratti, badly," he said testily. "I was lenient when it came to pot, but that kid was dealing ecstasy and deserved to go to jail."

"How long was she inside?"

"Two years, eight months. But now she's out and, as you can see, she's found work."

"You got her the job, didn't you?"

"I know her mother. She owns a little laundromat. My wife's been her client for years."

I took a bite of my *pastina di riso*. Exquisite stuff. You ask me, pastries that good can only be found in Padua and Verona.

"Were you joking about Zorzi being rich or did you find hard evidence?"

"His partner earns a little more than 800 euro a month working part-time at a tailor, but, turns out, she owns three large apartments that she rents to university students. Three hundred a month for a bed."

"Making the most of hard-earned savings."

"As I see it, Pellegrini was paying him cash in hand. I'll leave it to you to find out why," he added, handing me a folded sheet of paper that contained all the information we needed to find the guy.

"You can count on us," I said.

I finished my cappuccino and stood up, but Campagna was quick. We stood face to face.

"Listen, Buratti, I have my own plan to get out of this fucked-up situation without winding up in jail or being kicked off the force, and you're not part of it."

"All right."

"I'll do what they ordered me to. And I want it to be clear that if you manage to screw over Dottoressa Marino, I'll be pleased to no end. But nothing is going to make me team up with three crooks."

"You made yourself clear. But we need to know what's going on at the station and what plot that witch is hatching. And you need to do us the favor of keeping us up to date. Otherwise we're hopeless."

"You're asking too much."

"You can't become Angela Marino's accomplice. You're as fond of her maneuvering as I am."

"It makes me shudder, Buratti, but she's my superior and we both serve the state."

"*And* Pellegrini. In the end he's the one who really stands to gain."

He stepped aside to let me pass.

Before leaving, I gave him a warning. "Don't put us in a position where we have nothing to lose. And stop insulting us. You're trying my patience."

The morning frost blotched the faces of the market vendors in Piazza della Frutta. The sun had put in a shy appearance, and many clients, especially the older ones, wouldn't risk sticking their noses out of the house.

I stopped at the café where I got my cigarettes. A couple packs and another coffee. The slot machines were all taken by people banking on the pipedream that they'd get lucky that morning. The kid behind the bar pointed at a woman in line at the cash register who was waiting to break a ten-euro bill.

"She's new," he said, "name's Nora. Has a studio apartment around the corner. She's Italian, and so are her clients. No blacks, no Moroccans, no Slavs. Rubbers mandatory."

The woman realized she was the subject of our conversation and turned so we could peep her profile. She wasn't young anymore and couldn't have been turning tricks for long.

"You her pimp?" I asked.

"Let's just say I'm helping her get on her feet."

The area was too central to be controlled by organized crews. Prostitution was tolerated if practiced with discretion for a limited period of time. Soon as the pursuit became remunerative, someone always came knocking.

The woman smiled awkwardly. In time she'd get the swing of it and her smile would become so fake that she could flaunt it, like her expert colleagues, a healthy dose of contempt for the men who paid to go to bed with her.

"Two cubs in the lion's den," I whispered to her young, green guardian.

He took offense and turned to another client, she went back to sliding coins into the slot machine, and I promised myself once again that I'd never set foot in that café.

The waiter at La Nena lived in a congested area on the city's east end, in a house built in the 1960s that looked as if it had been designed by a child. Blocky, simple, basic. It needed a new paint job; the walls were a depressing shade of gray. It stood in the middle of a large green space, partly occupied by a prefab garage and partly by a well-tended kitchen garden.

We should have staked the place out, studied the man's movements, and chosen the right moment to approach him, but it was too cold, and for some reason we felt protected by the cops. If Zorzi complained, we could always justify ourselves by dragging in Campagna and Dottoressa Marino.

So all three of us showed up at his gate, ringing the bell with zeal. The waiter usually left for work at that hour, but the restaurant was still closed, and there was no sign that he'd found a new job.

One of the curtains fluttered; I pressed down on the doorbell.

A little later the door opened and the man approached. He was bundled up in a designer down jacket but all he had on his feet were brown rubber clogs. He couldn't have been taller than five-seven, not fat, not skinny, an unremarkable face.

"What do you want?" he asked in dialect.

"Why don't you let us in?" asked Rossini politely.

"I know you," he said. "I saw you at La Nena. What do you want?"

He wasn't ruffled. He knew perfectly well who we were, and yet we hadn't set foot in La Nena more than two or three times. I shot my partners a look, then improvised. "You used to be Pellegrini's right-hand man. He slipped you an extra cut. Till now things were going your way, but we need some information."

"I don't know anything," he interrupted.

I shook my head and stared him in the eye. "As I was saying, we can make your life hell and call the cops in to interrogate you about how you managed to buy those apartments that you rent to students."

He didn't bother to respond. He remained unruffled. While he listened, he looked us over, his head at a slight tilt.

"Tell us what you know and we'll leave you be," Max added calmly.

I'd come across guys like Zorzi before. Anonymous, nothing about them to pique your interest. Silent, always knew their place. But scratch the surface and you begin to realize you're dealing with hard-asses who think like seasoned gangsters, because that's what they've always been, and no one ever bothered to notice.

Old Rossini had already sized him up and changed tack. "You were good at going undetected. And we want to treat you with the respect you deserve. You don't owe Pellegrini anything anymore. The restaurant's closed and won't reopen. We're investigating the murders of Martina and Gemma, and we know how close you were to them."

Only then did Zorzi's face betray a dash of humanity. "The ladies were good people, kind. They listened to me."

"It was Giorgio Pellegrini who told you to keep an eye on them, wasn't it?" asked Beniamino, treading lightly. "At first he took care of it, but then he passed on the task to you because you were the only one he trusted."

The waiter nodded and Rossini seized on the opening. "Help us find the killers. We're not cops. If we find them, we'll make them pay."

"Giorgio said you guys are bad business," he said, gauging our reactions. "That you've got unfriendly intentions."

"If I find him I'll kill him," admitted Beniamino. "But we're not interested in him right now. We want to get hold of the pieces of shit who tortured, raped, and killed the two ladies."

"Your friends threatened me," Zorzi pointed out. "They owe me an apology."

"You're right, they don't know how to conduct themselves, because they're not professionals," Beniamino explained. "But you and I are, we understood one another immediately."

Satisfied, the man snorted and picked out a key from a rather voluminous ring. He led us into a large living room heated by a majolica stove. The wife must have done the decorating; chintzy as it was, it had personality. Looking around, I realized that while the exterior of the house appeared as modest as its owner, every last detail of the interior smacked of luxury.

He signaled for us to take the couch and sat down on an armchair opposite.

He didn't offer us anything and came straight to the point. "The person you're looking for is a woman," he said flatly. "I noticed her the first time she came to lunch at La Nena. She looked distracted, but nothing escaped her notice. Plus she didn't take her eyes off the two ladies. Not in a conspicuous way, but I caught it. I figured she was either a cop or a spy."

"The restaurant was always full. How did you notice her?" I asked.

He smiled. "Scoping people out was my job. Giorgio paid me to identify personae non gratae."

"Even after he fled?" I asked.

"That's none of your fucking business."

I didn't press him; his answer was more than sufficient.

"How many times did the woman come to the restaurant?" asked Max.

"A couple of lunches, often during happy hour, and dinner on odd days the first week, even days the second. By the third week she was gone. On Wednesday the women were murdered."

"Can you describe her?"

He pulled a phone out of his pants pocket. "I can do better than that. I took two photos," he replied casually. "I showed them to the ladies so that they knew not to talk to her. But it was too late. She'd already feigned an interest in the old building and gotten them to show her the cellar."

That dispelled any lingering doubts about the mystery woman; clearly she was the scout working for the killers.

It was the wrong question, but I couldn't keep my mouth shut: "Why didn't you give the photos to the police?"

He stared at me a moment with a disgusted look on his face, then started swiping through the photos on his phone.

The phone was passed around, and when it came around to me I found myself looking at a close-up of a forty-something with short jet-black hair. Her eyes were black too. Her face was round, full, olive-skinned. She wore too much makeup, bold lipstick that didn't suit her. My guard was up, because I was positive she'd paved the way for the killers, but, despite my resistance, I had to admit she was attractive. In the other image she was standing. She wasn't tall but well proportioned. She wore designer clothes, strictly black save for her shoes, a pair of beige pumps with a real high heel.

It was a fair guess that the clothes were a far cry from what she normally wore. I wondered about her actual tastes. Zorzi asked Rossini for his number so that he could send him the photos, and Rossini sent them to us.

The waiter stood up. "I'll walk you out," he said icily. A last courtesy. That was all the help we'd get from him.

As Zorzi was about to shut the double-lock gate, Rossini turned around to shake his hand. "Thank you and good-bye," he said, making it clear that we wouldn't trouble him again.

Back in the car I let him have it: "Since when do we defer to a guy who works for Pellegrini?"

As Beniamino lit a cigarette, his shirt cuff slipped down, bringing his bracelets into full view. "Sometimes good manners get you further than threats. Besides, that guy's bad news. We're better off not making enemies with him."

I sent the photos of the mysterious woman to Campagna along with a message: "Need ID."

The Fat Man sighed. "It would have been easier to kill the ladies in their apartment. Instead the killers wanted to avail themselves of the cellar to buy themselves time and muffle the noise."

"So?"

"Two considerations. The first we know already: strangling them on Pellegrini's turf was symbolic. The second is that the pretty brunette in the photo picked the place. She's not a scout, she's a boss. I bet she participated in the killings. Forensics found a size eight footprint."

"Maybe she's a smaller size," I thought out loud, studying the feet of the girl on my phone. "But an insole and thick socks are all you need to wear a shoe that suggests a man and not a woman was there."

"You're right, Max," the Old Gangster agreed. "She acted like she ran the operation. She checked out places, alternatives, escape routes. Clearly she's the kind of person who doesn't trust anybody. But I don't get why she let herself be seen so many times in the restaurant. In the end someone noticed her, and now we know what she looks like."

"It was a risk she had to take if she wanted to have everything under control," speculated the Fat Man.

"Or else this was personal," I hazarded, "and she wanted to expose herself to settle a score with Handsome Giorgio. We all know Pellegrini has a real talent for making people want to kill him."

"Motives aside, I'm sure Pellegrini knows her," said Beniamino. "If Campagna can't ID the woman, we can always ask Marino to show Pellegrini the photo."

I turned around to gauge his expression. Not a hint of irony. "You're joking, right?"

He shook his head. "No."

"Depends how we ask," continued Rossini.

"You want to trigger a war with the wicked witch?" I asked, stunned.

"We've got to get it through to her that if she wants to nail us on this, it won't be easy."

He sensed my perplexity.

"We're not aboveboard, Marco. Much less cops. We don't think like them. And that difference could save our ass."

"I'd like to remind you that Marino is ready to pin three kilos of cocaine on us whenever the spirit moves her."

"Well, seeing as she had the decency to tell us what crime she plans to pin on us, we ought to pick up the pace."

I had to agree, yet I was still praying to the gods that Campagna could ID the woman.

A few minutes later the inspector called with disappointing news. "All the powerful means at my disposal won't allow me to adequately search for this woman."

"Ask Marino."

The detective dropped the call without another word.

"On to Plan B," I said to the Old Gangster.

I rang again. "Don't hang up, Campagna."

"You're wasting my time, Buratti."

"What are you talking about? They took you off all your cases," I shot back. "You don't want me complaining to the Dottoressa, do you?"

"What do you want?" he huffed.

"Is Marino in Padua?"

"Maybe," he answered suspiciously.

"Where do I find her?"

"At the station."

I lost my cool. "How long are we going to play this little game?"

"First you tell me why you want to know where she lives."

"We need to talk to her."

"I'll relay the message. Maybe."

That time, I hung up.

"What a dick!" I hissed.

"The more they fuck him over, the tighter he clings to his badge," remarked Beniamino.

Max had worked up an appetite. He mentioned a restaurant in the area known for *baccalà alla vicentina*, but it was too early to sit down to eat, so he took out a few sheets of notebook paper from his inside pocket. "We're going shopping," he announced.

Old Rossini and I protested, but the Fat Man wouldn't budge. "We've got nothing at home and I'm always the one stocking up on supplies. Only seems fair that I take advantage of this moment when we're all together."

Beniamino made a clumsy attempt to wiggle his way out of it. "I don't live with you."

"It's true. You go back to your place a couple of days each week," said Max.

I peeped the list. "One cart won't do the trick, am I right?"

The Fat Man chuckled. "Afraid not."

An hour later we stepped out of the supermarket loaded up like packhorses, ventured into the large parking garage, and found Campagna leaning against Beniamino's sedan, his arms crossed and a wry look on his face.

"How'd you find us?" I asked, though I already knew the answer.

"I'm good."

"Whose phone are you tracing?"

"Yours."

"Bullshit," said Beniamino icily. "An hour tops before we pop your balloon."

"If I were you I might also have a look at this pretty little car," suggested the detective.

Giulio Campagna was a complicated man.

"Why?" I asked.

"Why what?"

"Why are you telling us your colleagues planted a tracking device on my friend's car?"

He raised his left thumb to list the reasons. "First, Marino's men aren't colleagues, they're dangerous aliens from distant galaxies deep in the Ministry of the Interior." He stuck out his index finger. "Second, I'd give the world to show you that while you might think you're criminal masterminds, you're really nothing more than three dumbfucks."

Beniamino clenched his fists and stepped forward, ready to land a right to the stomach and a left to the chin. I'd seen him do it before. Campagna was expecting it and pulled his gun out in time. Luckily, he didn't point it at him.

"Don't try it," he muttered. "A crook hasn't laid a hand on me my entire career."

"I'll ram that toy up your ass," replied Beniamino, entirely unfazed. "That'll teach you to act properly."

I stepped between them. "Put the piece away," I demanded. "Thanks for the heads-up, but as I already pointed out to you, you have a bad habit of casting nasty aspersions. And not everybody is as forgiving as I am."

The standard-issue Beretta was returned to its holster.

"Let's talk about serious matters," said Campagna, keeping an eye on Old Rossini. "If you succeed in creating a channel to Marino, I'm happy. The farther away from this mess I am, the better my chances of getting out of it. But clearly I can't give you information about her. She'd immediately know it was me."

"So then?" I asked.

"I'll show you the road and you take it from there."

"And where would this road happen to lead?"

"To Sergeant Francesco Marmorato and Special Agent Lorenzo Pitta. They're her shadows."

Marmorato had greeted me with a pat down when I'd met Marino. Pitta must have been the driver. But I'd barely glimpsed the guy and wouldn't be able to recognize him.

"They're posted at the barracks in Celere and eat dinner nearby at Cosimo's," he explained. "The owner, Cosimo Stella, is Marmorato's *compaesano.*"

"Sounds like this road's all uphill," I remarked.

The inspector shrugged. "You should be grateful. Anyway, I heard they're serving spaghetti and sardines tonight."

I pressed him for more details. "What else have you heard? Why are those three stationed in Padua? What's going on?"

"They don't tell me anything, Buratti," he admitted bitterly. "I overheard them mention the restaurant when they were chatting by the coffee machine."

He waved us goodbye and walked off.

I looked at my friends. Max's face had turned to stone. "You didn't say peep," I observed.

"You know I don't talk to that guy. Once was enough."

"I don't want anything to do with him either," added Rossini with rancor. "He had the nerve to pull his gun on us. He's a pig at heart."

I laughed to ease the tension. "I get it. Campagna is my cross to bear."

Beniamino winked at the Fat Man. "For some reason these two understand one another."

"Right. Deep down they like each other," said Max.

I didn't reply because it was true. Maybe I understood the deep unease that kept the cop up at night.

"We'll have to postpone lunch," I announced. "Replacing our cell phones is more urgent."

"We should get a clean phone for Campagna too," suggested Max.

Right. Clearly his phone was being tapped too. "Let's hope he doesn't make a fuss about it," I said.

"But we should leave the tracking device where it is and change cars," said the Old Gangster. "They already know this one and they'd just keep planting new ones in it."

Max laughed. "I thought you just wanted to use Marco's Škoda Felicia."

Rossini feigned indignation. "I've got a reputation to uphold. There are some clunkers I can't be seen in. Besides, that car's not safe anymore either."

The Fat Man insisted on tending to the groceries first, which he arranged with methodical precision. Finally we hit the road for Mantua, where we bought new SIM cards using the names of unwitting clients from another store.

Then we drove across Veneto in the opposite direction. We left the sedan in the parking lot of the hospital in Mestre and continued by bus to Dario Tomasella's body shop in a small village outside Treviso. For a while now Dario had been in business with a Romanian gang that hustled stolen cars on the Eastern European market. He and his loyal employees were tasked with retrofitting them on the fly for the trip across the border.

Dario was an old friend from prison and, at sixty, had no intention of becoming a guest of the state again. He'd become shrewder, quit gambling away his money, and only conducted business with people he held in high regard.

Beniamino and I were in that category, and he was happy to see us. Before talking business, he invited us to the bar to knock back a bottle of good Prosecco.

He started gossiping about the local racket, and we were forced to tell him that we were in a hurry.

"What kind of vehicle will do you?" he asked.

"It's got to be clean," replied Rossini. "Ours are out of commission for a while."

"No problem. I have two courtesy cars available that I got off a colleague who shuttered his business," explained the mechanic. "Two hundred a day and they're yours for as long as you like."

"That's way above market price. A hundred and fifty for the two," I countered.

He sighed. "I've got to get used to the fact that the good old days, when criminals didn't haggle over prices and just handed over a wad of bills in their pocket, are never coming back."

To take the sting out of his nostalgia, we uncorked another bottle before finally leaving for Padua aboard two small Toyotas the color of cheap wine.

The two cops didn't enter Da Cosimo until around 9:30, taking their time. I waited until they'd had a glass of wine and then made my way over. Pitta, Marino's driver, saw me first and poked Marmorato's arm. Marmorato looked up from his cellphone.

I kept my hands in plain sight to signal that I didn't have any ill intentions. Judging from the look on their faces, they were clearly surprised, but they came to their senses in no time. According to the plan, I was supposed to appear calm and collected, at most play dumb. In truth I feared the worst, that they'd haul me off to the tank so that I'd think twice about spoiling dinner for the next guy in uniform.

"Sorry for sneaking up on you like this," I began, speaking softly.

"How'd you know we were here?" barked Marmorato, who could draw no other conclusion than that we knew too much about their business.

"This is my town," I replied flatly.

"What's that supposed to mean?" asked Pitta.

I didn't bother answering him and stared at the sergeant until I got the question I was after.

"What the fuck did you come here for, Buratti?"

"I need to talk with the Dottoressa. It's urgent."

"Communication of that kind, you've got to go through Inspector Campagna. I thought that was clear."

"Campagna doesn't count for jack shit," I replied dryly.

Pitta gestured to me to piss off. "Get lost, asshole. We'll see you at the station tomorrow."

I didn't move. "I said it's urgent."

The two cops exchanged a look. Marmorato stood up and left to make a call. A waiter arrived with two plates of steaming pasta. The cop snatched up his fork but after a second slammed it on the table. "I can't eat with your ugly mug looking at me."

That was the second time he'd insulted me. The tension was killing me, and arguing would have done me good, but now wasn't the time. There was no way for me to check it. I kept quiet and scoped out the other tables. I trained my eyes on a group of women in their forties talking intensely. They were clearly intimate, must have known each other a long time. And they had the same hairdresser, apparently: their hair had been cut and dyed by the same hand.

Marmorato signaled for me to join him outside. He was red in the face and shaking with the desire to kick my ass. Marino must have chewed him out. He handed me the phone.

"Good evening, Dottoressa."

"You can't afford to pull these *guappo* stunts, Buratti."

"What are you talking about?"

"You know. Stay away from my men."

"I didn't hurt anyone. I took the liberty of interrupting their dinner because I was in a hurry to talk to you."

"How did you know they'd be eating there?"

"Maybe they're not as smart as you think."

She burst into laughter. "Whereas you're the slickest of them all, right?"

The moment had come to drop the verbal sparring. This cop was far more agile than me.

"Why don't you ask me why I tracked you down?"

"Because I'm sure your reasons are half-assed," she replied arrogantly. "You just wanted to demonstrate that you and your little friends have a few tricks up your sleeves."

"You're wrong, Dottoressa, I just do as I'm told," I shot back. "I have in my possession a photo of the person who planned the murder of Pellegrini's women and I need to put a name to it in order to continue the investigation. But you must know that already, seeing as you're tapping Inspector Campagna's phone."

Angela Marino got quiet. This time I'd managed to impress her, to show her that we weren't lambs for slaughter.

I saw my opening. "It shouldn't be too hard for you to ID the girl. Handsome Giorgio must know her. Maybe he pissed her off. That's his M.O., after all."

"O.K., you're not as dumb as I'd thought," the detective huffed. "Cut to the chase."

The time had come to speak frankly.

"You're hiding information from the mobile squad, otherwise we'd have come across different intel in the file and the woman would have already had a warrant out on her," I said flatly. "You found a way to get my friends and I to find her all on our own to avoid having someone come along and accuse you of not having informed the lead investigators."

"You're in no position to question how we operate."

I ignored her. The Dottoressa was getting irritated.

"We want to know why it's important for us to follow this lead and find Martina and Gemma's killers."

"Or else?"

"Or else we're lacking the proper motivation."

"You fuckhead. Did you ask yourself why I'm not worried about you going to the press or delivering documents to some lawyer or notary?"

"Because whatever operation Giorgio Pellegrini is involved in," I replied, "is worth more than our miserable lives. And the lives of Pellegrini's wife and mistress, which were sacrificed at the altar of the state's superior concerns. But we're outlaws, and we've got nothing to do with your intrigues."

"I think it's a little late for statements of principles."

"You're right. We've been blackmailed into wading through your muck, but we're talking about survival plain and simple. Soon as the situation allows, we go our separate ways."

"You're not going anywhere."

I abstained from answering. We'd both made ourselves clear.

"This time I need an answer, Dottoressa: why is it important for us to find that woman?"

"Because she disappeared," she explained in that icy voice of hers. "We don't know where she's gone, and she represents a threat to Pellegrini's life."

And to the life of the operation, I thought.

"Now let my men eat in peace," she ordered before hanging up.

I handed Marmorato back his phone and walked off, trailed for a few feet by his insults. Beniamino and Max were waiting for me a short distance away in the car.

"How'd it go?" asked the Fat Man. Rossini offered me a smoke.

"I've got no idea," I responded in all honesty. "I got it

through to her that we won't willingly be played, and she made it clear, in that elegant way of hers, that she couldn't give a flying fuck."

"What did she say about the brunette who slaughtered the two ladies?" asked the Old Gangster.

"That we have to find her to protect Handsome Giorgio and his bullshit schemes. I'm confident the Dottoressa will feed us some useful information through Campagna."

"I'm hungry," complained Max. "I want a decent meal and I don't feel like cooking."

"But the fridge is full!" cried Rossini, winking at me.

"Today's not the day," pointed out the Fat Man bitterly. "I wouldn't be able to really express myself in the kitchen."

I took Rossini up on his invitation to have a goof and turned anxiously to Max. "Do you think you've taken this celebrity chef fad a bit too far?"

He gave me a vexed look and launched into a tirade about foodie culture. Listening to him talk was a pleasure. Max the Memory is an insightful, cultured man. And passionate. I loved and continue to love him, and I wished he would dig himself out of the profound acrimony that he buried by binging on food. But being on the losing side exacted a hefty toll.

We drove on a few miles, crossed the bridge over the Bacchiglione, and slipped down the roads that flanked the river.

Sauro Trincanato was a disgraced cook. Drunk every night, he'd torched the reputation of his restaurant and chased off a clientele that had no qualms about spending money. Now the bottle was nothing but a bad memory. He'd been saved by AA, but he still didn't have the strength to open another restaurant and face the city's critics. Every night he cooked for whoever knocked on the door of his little house, which his wife had, by some miracle, managed to save from his creditors. In the large basement he'd set up an old-fashioned osteria. There was a single table several feet long where friends and old clients were seated. The place was no frills. Afterward you left on the table whatever payment you thought proper.

I was happy to go there. I wasn't particularly fond of Sauro, but you ate well, and the place was lively. I always liked lending a hand to people who took a second stab at life. All the world does is bare its teeth, and humanity has become a rare commodity. Plus his wife had a good sense of humor and was always a pleasure to talk to.

I bumped into Maurizio Camardi, my saxophonist friend just back from recording. Next to him sat Francesco Garolfi, a guitar player from Lombardy possessed by the blues. They recommended the pumpkin soup with chestnuts and speck. I tendered a bottle of Marchese di Villamarina, a cabernet sauvignon harvested in the late fall in Alghero, on the vast estates of Sella & Mosca.

A couple of patrons drew Max and Beniamino into the usual debate about the future of the country, while we talked music and musicians. I used to be part of the scene, back when I sang with the Old Red Alligators. Then my voice dried up in jail and I didn't sing another note. Maurizio knew my story and had the tact not to embarrass me. At first I believed I'd go insane, seeing as the entire seven years that I spent behind bars I was sure I would return to performing, to touring Europe with my blues. Prison deprives you of more than just your freedom, and to survive you have to gnaw off a piece of life you'd once held dear. My punishment was disproportionate; aside from my voice, it had taken away the woman I loved.

That's how it went. Jail had done a number on Max and Beniamino too. And I couldn't do anything about it except act like I didn't give a fuck because I'd learned to live in the world. Instead I continued being a goddamn beginner.

Camardi and Garolfi got their instruments out of their cases and launched into a cover all their own of "Foxy Lady."

Old Jimi Hendrix would have approved.

The following morning Beniamino woke me up by banging on the door.

"That fucking pig is waiting for you in the living room."

"Who?"

"Campagna."

I pulled on a shirt and pants, and a few minutes later I was sitting face to face with the inspector. "Coming here wasn't a good idea," I said, ticked off. "Rossini hasn't forgotten. Keep your distance."

The detective pretended not to hear me. "It's 9:45. Respectable people are already at work by now."

He was exasperating. "You want a coffee, Campagna?" I asked, making my way to the kitchen.

He nodded and followed me. "What the hell did you do last night? The Dottoressa and her boys were pretty pissed this morning."

I held up the various capsules of coffee. "What kind do you want?"

"Whichever," he replied. "All of a sudden everyone's an expert. You used to drink whatever dirt was on sale at the supermarket, then a Hollywood star comes along and everybody's talking roasts and blends."

While Campagna let off steam I ran a hand over my face and thought about the pleasure I'd take in a shave as soon as he left. Who knows what he'd say if he discovered my weakness for shaving with a soap and brush.

As was his habit, he abruptly changed the subject.

"The Dottoressa ID'd the woman in the photo. Her name is Paz Anaya Vega, born in Santa Cruz de Tenerife on April 4, 1979."

"That all?"

"No. But first I want to know if it's true you told those morons Marmorato and Pitta that yours truly doesn't count for jack shit. That's the first thing they rubbed my nose in this morning."

"I did you a favor," I lied.

Campagna sneered. "'Your informant is convinced you don't count for jack shit.' Their exact words."

"Careful who you're calling an informant. Besides, you really don't count for jack shit," I snapped. "May I remind you that according to the Dottoressa's plans we're both looking at years in jail."

He wagged his finger in my face. "As usual you're fucking clueless," he scolded. "Their ridicule made me realize how they'll try to prove you and I are connected. You were my snitch and then we partnered up."

At last I got it, the latest ploy in Angela Marino's diabolical mind. If I ended up branded a rat in jail, my life would be hell. It was an old trick to help convince any holdouts that they ought to collaborate.

"Her goal is to get you to pen the *Life, Death, and Miracles of Saint Rossini*."

"I know."

"You know what scares me about that woman?"

I had no idea. "The list is long."

"Her strategic vision for the investigation. I've never met anyone with her capacity to imagine the future, to never content herself with quick results."

Cop on cop admiration. I was tired of his chatter and turned the conversation back around to the Spaniard. "What can you tell me about Paz Anaya Vega?"

"Legacy case. Her father headed up a band of drug traffickers in Madrid until the Georgian mafia took him out in 2006," he began. "Paz vanished after the funeral and a lot of people were convinced that she'd wound up under a pile of rubble. But in 2012 she resurfaces in Vienna on the arm of Tobias Slezak, an ex-mercenary who'd fought with the Croatians and who, in the early 2000s, set up a small organization of drug dealers.

"After Paz shows up everything changes. She has the right contacts—Galician wholesalers who import cocaine from South America—and the quality of their product spikes. In no time she and Tobias are running an operation small in size but big in profit.

"They have no intention of expanding the business because they don't want to run into trouble with the mafia clans that have divvied up Austria for a long time now. Everything's going gangbusters until, once again, death, with all its destructive force, comes knocking at the pretty Spaniard's door."

"What happened?"

"About a year ago her man was murdered and she went on the lam. According to her Austrian colleagues she fled the country. Maybe she went back to Spain."

"Who killed Slezak?"

The inspector frowned. "Marino ordered me to tell you what I've told you. I don't know anything else, and I don't care to."

"It's eating away at you. You can tell just by looking at you."

"That woman doesn't know the meaning of respect. Humiliates me in front of my colleagues," he confessed. "Just be patient. All things pass. Even the Dottoressa will turn out to be nothing but a bad memory."

Keep dreaming, I wanted to tell him, but I restrained myself. Campagna was increasingly distraught, and I couldn't wait for him to leave.

I took a clean phone out of the drawer. "I know it's illegal, but yours is being tapped by Angela Marino's goons, and we need to be able to talk in peace."

I held it out. After hesitating a moment, he took it.

"They're not stupid," he said. "They'll figure out we're going behind their backs."

"They have to start assuming that we're not stupid either."

He stared at me. "You sure about this, Buratti?"

"They outman us is all."

"I should hope so. They represent the state."

"A perverse bit of it."

For once he fell silent. He put the phone in the pocket of his parka and headed for the door.

I found my friends back in the kitchen. Max making a sumptuous breakfast, Rossini reading the paper.

"You tell that pig never to set foot in this house again?" asked the Fat Man combatively.

"Yes. But you can never be too sure with Campagna. Besides, he's a pig. They come and go as they please."

Beniamino folded up the paper. "Any news?"

I filled them in while heating up some milk and nabbing a couple slices of buttered toast with jam, which the Fat Man had prepared with the assiduousness of a monk.

"Marino has left no stone unturned," grumbled Max. "It's clear she knows a lot more about this whole affair than she let on."

"She doesn't want to risk having someone turn up one day accusing her of using us, of giving us classified information. She's held back everything but what we would have discovered for ourselves with a bit of time on our hands."

Max turned on the tablet and opened Google. Austrian media had followed the story for several days.

"Tobias Slezak and two of his bodyguards were murdered in Vienna in an apartment in the Brigittenau neighborhood," reported the Fat Man. "Four kilos of cocaine were discovered next to the bodies. Several witnesses who heard shots fired said they saw a lone man run from the building. The police have released an identikit."

Max turned the screen around so we could see the photo. "Recognize anyone familiar?" he asked triumphantly.

"Christ, it's Pellegrini," cried Old Rossini.

There was no doubt about it. It was him all right. Now we could at least piece together part of the story.

Giorgio Pellegrini had fled Padua pursued by a warrant for his arrest and Rossini's pledge to turn him into another bracelet to vaunt on his wrist. Somehow he had entered into contact with Slezak's organization, probably with the intention of inserting himself into the drug-trafficking ring: life on the run comes at a price and there's never enough money. But, just as he was finalizing the deal, tempers must have flared, and he fired first, killing three men and once again vanishing into thin air. Pellegrini is vile, but you have to give him credit: His knack for disappearing is extraordinary. He has a nose for danger and always has a ready backup plan.

Paz Anaya Vega, Slezak's wife and one of the organization's heavies, also went underground, right after the funeral. But she wasn't on the run. She was on the hunt. She wanted to find Giorgio Pellegrini and exact revenge. And she began settling accounts by killing the wife and mistress.

"It doesn't make sense," balked Max. "Why didn't Pellegrini take the coke? It was worth a fortune on the market."

Old Rossini chimed in: "We've got to find out whether he was already on the pigs' dole in Vienna."

"Can't be ruled out," I said. "To inherit the Eden of immunity, Pellegrini's capable of anything."

Max opened the fridge and came up with a jar of yogurt. "So we're talking about an execution. For some motive that we're overlooking right now, it was imperative that those three guys die."

"Another good reason for the Spaniard to flee the scene. She was scared she'd meet the same end."

"But her desire for vengeance drove her to Padua, to hang around the victims, to kill them in that flagrant way. And that," I objected, "was a gamble."

"Yeah," said Rossini, cutting me off, "but a tiny one. From an operational standpoint it was perfect."

"According to Dottoressa Marino it's our job to track down Paz Anaya Vega and her men."

"She wants to make sure this doesn't get too close to Pellegrini," said Beniamino, running a finger over his bracelets. "At the same time she wants to collect evidence of a connection between us and the drug dealers to present in court."

"And the star witness will be none other than Pellegrini," I added. "She'll enjoy the show from the rafters."

Max sighed with disdain. "The grand puppeteer."

We smoked in silence, lost in thought. My friends' faces were grim.

"Do we know anybody in Vienna?" I asked, sick of spooling through nightmares of my future as a jailbird.

The Old Gangster nodded. "Pierino Martinenghi."

"You sure?" asked Max, surprised. "Didn't he move to Denmark?"

"That didn't last long. Now he works at a hotel and dines on Sachertorte."

"He works?"

"He's gotten wise. Doesn't want to attract the attention of the local authorities. But he still has a thing for safes."

I glanced at my watch and asked the Fat Man to check when the next train departed for the Austrian capital.

THREE

I couldn't pick them out, but I sensed their presence. Serj Balakian's men were spying on me. It was the fourth time that the Armenian had arranged a meet, through contacts who took their sweet ass time, and then was a no-show.

I paid the bill and headed off in the direction of Kapuzinerplatz, prompting disappointed looks on the faces of two old gals. The whole time they'd been making eyes at me while I had to sit tight in that shitty posh patisserie. They weren't bad. They oozed money and class. Were circumstances different I'd have taken advantage of the situation, showed them I was available, a gentleman, and at the same time open-minded, would have suggested we split a little something three ways with a surprise ending that only I'd have appreciated. They'd have been so shaken up that they would have stopped seeing one another and tried to forget what had happened with that charming and apparently harmless man. So "normal." Not even the best shrink would have given them answers, while I would have retained only happy memories of the permanent scars that I'd left on their lives.

I bid the women goodbye with a regretful smile. It had been a minute since I'd had myself some fun, but the situation wouldn't allow it. All eyes were on me. The eyes of Italian cops and international crooks. I'd get another shot. It was just a matter of being patient. According to a bank LED display, it was ten degrees out. The cold didn't bother me, but it had spoiled my stay in Munich, and I couldn't wait to get out of there. I'd been in the city for over a month and a half and was growing bored.

Balakian would eventually decide to meet me, but, for my tastes, it would be too late. I entered a department store and lost my two shadows, a man and a woman who had been trailing me since Tumblingerstraße and had done nothing to avoid being noticed.

I had to show Balakian that I wasn't Sucker Number One. Besides, I didn't feel like advertising my home address.

Angelina Marino was the one who procured my apartment, a cranny in Neuperlach. She'd put me up in a two-bedroom, furnished with scrap merch, on the first floor of a building two blocks from Kafkastraße.

I deserved better, but Marino was cheap. She believed even special operations needed to curb expenses.

A bitch with few equals, that cop, but she was the only one who understood that I could come in handy for complicated missions with multiple layers, the fruit of long and grueling meetings. So, when I put myself on the immunity market, she proposed something that, on the face of it, might have seemed like a suicide mission. In reality, it was the wet dream of ministry heavies, but before I came along they couldn't find volunteers among the crooks for hire, and as far as I knew they'd sacrificed a pair of agents for nothing in an attempt to infiltrate Balakian's organization. Which wasn't even the main objective, only a means to touch someone whose identity they still didn't know.

Marino was still buttoned up. She didn't trust me. Even though, just to make myself appetizing to the guy, I'd had to kill three drug-traffickers in Vienna. For over four months I'd had to pretend I was a coke buyer looking for a wholesaler with no ties to Italy. Angela had made me memorize a little story about a fallout with the mafia. A half-baked tale only delinquent Austrians would buy, industry outsiders unaccustomed to a certain class of con. Like being shot while receiving a briefcase full of money for four kilos of cocaine. They were former mercenaries who thought all you had to do to stay alive was follow procedure. They couldn't conceive of someone not giving a shit about rules of engagement. They checked out the references given to them by a regular customer they didn't know was being blackmailed by Interpol. They wanted to meet me. On the street, in a café, at a restaurant. And then at a brothel. How typical. Finally they wanted to see the money. That wasn't the way things were supposed to be done, but because I wanted to prove I was a reliable customer, I humored them. Wads of cash from the maze of ministry slush funds.

One week of silence and then out of nowhere they summon me to an apartment, the kind rented out to tourists or for special events. But because I had taken the precaution of not using a cellphone and could only be found at a certain joint I stopped by every night at the same hour, Tobias Slezak was compelled to give me the address in person the evening before the meet. It was a minor breach of protocol, but protocol should never be breached. The boss was sure he wasn't running any risks; after all, they'd checked me out thoroughly. He failed to realize that he had fallen victim to overconfidence, which in the world of crime must be avoided like the plague. So, while he and his men slept like angels and dreamed of the rustle of banknotes that I was supposed to hand over the following morning, I slipped into the apartment—shut with a ridiculous lock—and hid a gun in each of the two bathrooms.

A classic. The same plan is narrated down to the last detail in *The Godfather*: After the attempt on his father's life, Michael Corleone meets rival boss Virgil Sollozzo and the corrupt police captain, McCluskey, in a restaurant in the Bronx. He lets them search him, feigning just the right amount of indignation, and then, after opening talks to broker a peace no one wants, he goes to take a leak. Once he's back at the table, he takes out a .38 caliber that had been taped behind the toilet, and lights them up with a couple shots to the head.

I did exactly what Corleone did. Introduced myself, let them frisk me, handed over the bag of money. They counted it while I sampled the cocaine, and then we had a drink. That's when I asked where the bathroom was. One of the two goons accompanied me to the nearest one. I took a Turkish-made 7.65 mm from under the sink and shot them both point-blank. First Slezak, then his goons. One apiece to the chest to put them out of commission, and the killshot to the head. The six shots made such a racket they attracted the attention of the usual busybodies. Lucky for me, the Viennese cops didn't care much about solving the case. When crooks kill crooks, public opinion and the media don't cry out for justice. Maybe Dottoressa Marino called in a favor, but I can't be sure.

My one regret was that Paz wasn't there. I'd have happily offed her. I'd been looking forward to that moment, paired it with fantasies befitting the disdain she'd shown me ever since we'd first met.

From the start she'd felt something about me didn't add up. She'd been brought up in Madrid's underworld and orphaned by Georgians—she was far more cunning than her man. She'd known every form of betrayal. She tried to persuade Slezak not to sell me the coke. Barring that, she demanded more background checks. But she had to capitulate: my candor outweighed her suspicions. I would have liked to have complimented her on her acumen. I was really bitter about missing the chance. The whore was dangerous, vindictive. She took her revenge on my girls to show me she was angry and determined but hadn't lost her head. She was lucid. She'd been able to keep her pain and rage under control. She wouldn't make a rash move; she would look for me as long as it took to find me and then do me harm. Real harm.

It's understandable, ultimately. For a woman at the head of an organization of drug-traffickers, however small, it's got to be tough losing the men in her life. First her father, then her partner.

I could have gotten rid of Paz when she'd shown up in Padua to plan the murders of Martina and Gemma. The moment I saw the photos that good-old Giampaolo Zorzi had taken, I was tempted to make a play on her, but it would have jeopardized the whole operation. To get close to Balakian I needed someone who wanted to eliminate me at all costs.

How the Spaniard discovered my name is Giorgio Pellegrini remained a mystery, but in the end that didn't matter much. I'd told Marino that photos of yours truly were circulating on the Internet, photos from my past, from my successful turn as a restaurateur, but she wasn't worried. She was sure that the identity that ministry experts had made for me was more than safe.

When they get the notion to act illegally, cops presume they're as wily as the most weathered crook. And the Dottoressa was no exception. She still hadn't realized that it isn't enough to know your target and ape his methods and habits. Not only is a crook's mindset completely different, so is the combination of instincts and impulses that drive him to crime.

To be honest, I'd have left Paz free to act anyway. It worked in my favor. For several reasons.

Martina and Gemma were creatures that I'd molded to suit my needs. I'd invested time, money, and energy in their training, and I wasn't about to let them become someone else's property. Plus, even without my guidance, cruel and empty unhappiness awaited them all the same. Death was no doubt the appropriate solution. Besides, I'd had to bid goodbye to La

Nena and Padua for good, and when you burn bridges you'd better not leave behind any encumbrances. And that's exactly what a wife and mistress are. On top of that, the double homicide offered me the possibility of settling the score with Buratti and Rossini. They were the ones, with the aid of that berserk pig Campagna, who forced me to flee Padua.

Angela Marino was enthusiastic about my offer to involve her in an unofficial investigation to track down the Spaniard who, in the meantime, had gone on the lam.

I called that fuckhead Buratti and he immediately took the bait. He knew Martina and Gemma, and I was sure that the pathetic frailty of Gemma had struck a nerve. He felt invested in the mission to free those two poor girls from my influence and thought he'd succeeded by forcing me to run. News of their death was a hard blow. It wasn't an accident that the lawyers he worked for called him the Crusader. I was sure he'd throw himself into the investigation to bring justice to those two poor innocent victims. Rossini the Relic and that fat fuck Max the Memory would have had his back.

Even if they were mixed up in "very" special operations, the police had to play dumb about what went down in Vienna, and having three crooks to sacrifice to the courts made things pretty cushy, especially if they fit the profile that would get the media's attention. Beniamino Rossini was born to play the role.

The three fuckheads had tried to save their asses by taking the most obvious shortcut: offing yours truly. But they were so crusty and unimaginative that predicting their next move was a piece of cake. After their third attempt I was sick of playing around and led them by the hand to the house where pretty Lotte Schlegel put me up. I liked that big girl—so Swiss, so subservient. She couldn't foresee that I was capable of taking her to dark places where she discovered she was happy to give up the dignity that poured out of her mouth. I felt kind of sorry for putting her down and stuffing her in that closet. But those three should have known that their attempts to kill me would trigger the death of more people. Plus I was irked when they started passing my photo around the slums of Bern. Getting other people involved is a punishable offense, an act of disloyalty. When I caught that guy snooping around Lotte's house, I knew the time had come to switch cities.

I followed that little nothing of a man and shot the breeze while he paused to drop five francs on the Swiss Lotto. Discovered his name was Hermann and that he'd worked for thirty years in Schwarzau Prison. In his pocket he had a couple of photographs that had appeared in a cooking magazine, and he recognized me. Had seen me in the neighborhood before, in the company of Lotte, and remembered me. He swore he'd met too many crooks in his lifetime not to recognize one on the street. Twaddle. I've got a gift for sizing up the greedy, the corrupt, so I paid him to sell me out to Buratti. I got him to give me one of the photos and taped it to the closet where the remains of my hostess hung. It seemed like a cute touch, one that would facilitate their finding her.

Marino lapped up my bullshit about Schlegel's homicide. I pinned the blame on Paz Anaya Vega, and when I complained about those three idiots' fruitless attempts to take my life, she didn't blink. She wanted to see the case through. Everything else, in her eyes, was mere detail. But I was sure that, despite her reassurances, she wanted to pull one over on me. It was foreseeable. In Italy certain things haven't changed since the dawn of time.

The state cut a deal with the mafia, arrested a boss, and squeezed those who did the dirty work, those who made the Cosa Nostra archive disappear. Some careers were torched after cases were brought with the sole aim of kicking up dust. Other people soared to the Mount Olympus of Power. The real kind. The kind that has always governed.

But unlike Paz, Marino didn't really get me. Beautiful

Angela, born and raised in the highest echelons of the Interior, tended to underestimate her enemies. Not only was she biased, more to the point, she couldn't hold back her disdain for moral degeneracy. Given her rank in the ministry, that attitude could have harmed her career in the long run. With me she'd made the same mistake. She was sure she was the sharper of the two, sure she could use me, trick me, and go back on her word.

But I'd make sure she didn't. I'm not the type to rot behind bars or go into hiding. In order to live large I had to go back to Italy and be among the well-heeled—presentable people, not necessarily saints. By now arrest warrants were the daily bread of people who ran business and politics. I had to go back to being considered a full-fledged citizen, with the right to vote and the obligation to pay taxes and bills. Only then could I devote myself to taking advantage of the corrupt and the weak.

Though I had yet to figure out how, I would force Angela Marino to behave accordingly. She still hadn't unveiled what I had to do after gaining Balakian's trust. No surprise, I was cooking up a plan to save myself right then.

To make sure I was finally alone, I walked into a famous, sprawling beer hall, tunneled past lively groups of Italian tourists—who came to Munich for the sole purpose of swilling beer—and escaped out the staff door that led to a back alley. I surprised two waiters smoking peacefully. I felt like smacking them around. No one who worked at a restaurant of mine would have taken the liberty. Breaks are for going to the bathroom. Then it's straight back to work. You only rest to eat. I felt like complaining to the director, bringing to his attention the fact that these two assholes would stink of smoke while serving food and drinks. But I let it go. My German is awful, and I didn't want to argue in English.

My phone rang. I didn't need to check who it was. It couldn't be anyone but Angela Marino.

"How'd it go?" she asked.

"Balakian was a no-show."

"He may not trust you yet, but if he continues to schedule meetings, it means he's interested."

"In money. Are you positive I'll have enough when the time comes?"

She scoffed. "We've gone over this already. Of course, if you could get your hands on the money you hid when you ran, it would lessen the burden on taxpayers."

"If I had any saved up, I'd live a more dignified life," I lied, "seeing as what you give me is outrageous."

She ignored me. "Buratti and his colleagues managed to identify Paz Anaya Vega and are now looking for her."

"I told you it was the Spaniard who killed my wife and her friend."

"You mean your girlfriend. Anyways, Pellegrini, I don't know shit until the mobile squad in Padua finds out the official truth."

Always ready to cover her own ass. "Is that all?"

"Do you have something better to do, Giorgio?" she asked in a fussy little squeak.

"I do," I said, and hung up.

She called back, but I didn't answer. Anger aroused certain fantasies in me, but I kept them at bay. Angela Marino may have been beautiful but she was the type of woman I couldn't get in sync with. There was no way to break her. Plus she was big stuff at PD. She was untouchable.

I slipped into a taxi as it was dropping someone off, rode out to Giesing and caught the subway to get home faster.

As I opened the door my nose picked up hints of almond and ginger. Perfume. My instinct told me to go introduce myself to whoever had taken a bath in the stuff. Despite everything, I didn't sense danger.

I entered the room and found the woman who'd been following me seated at the kitchen table. Her long jacket was folded perfectly and slung over the back of a chair. With her left index finger she pointed to the couch.

She was thin, her face outrageously chiseled, her skin pulled back against the bone. But she wasn't ill, much less anorexic. Her tightfitting shirt amplified her toned arms and threw her little muscles in relief. She was one of those women who kills herself on the rowing machine to get back at Mother Nature. Were she not so ugly I'd have given her a workout myself.

"Where's your friend?" I asked in English, removing my jacket. "Hiding in the tub?"

She smiled, amused. "No, he's outside. In case there's trouble."

I collapsed onto the uncomfortable pillows of the couch. "You smell nice."

She shook her head. "What, this? Barely passable. I wear it when I work."

A real joker, this broad. "Am I supposed to congratulate you for tailing me all the way to this house?"

"We've known the address for a month," she explained, the smartass. "We've searched it more than a few times. You never even realized, did you?"

"No," I confessed.

"You're not very good at covering your tracks either," she went on, unfazed, as if to scold me. "You always take the same route. And you're cocky. Almost smug. Indiscreet, given the dangerous situation you're in . . . Mr. Sforza."

Attilio Sforza. The identity that those geniuses at special ops had cooked up for me along with an appropriate cover story and a respectable criminal CV. But I hated the name. It sounded fake. And now I was wondering if this woman was harboring doubts about it too.

I pretended to be embarrassed. "I thought I was better than that."

The woman just stared at me. Then she decided to disclose

the reason for her visit. "After every meeting we've arranged, you receive a phone call. The same happened today. We want to know who you're talking to."

Hats off to Balakian's organization! They were real professionals, left nothing to chance. But I'm the king of liars and managed to parry her blow with a plausible story—a classic.

"A woman I'm very fond of."

She cocked her eyebrow, an expression that looked unnatural and slightly ridiculous on her. But the broad wasn't stupid; she took all the time she needed to absorb my answer. She held out her hand. "Cell phone," she ordered.

I stood up and handed it to her with a cooperative, solicitous air. I was trying to fuck her in the ass with a bucket of Vaseline, but I could picture how this would end.

She checked it and made no comment when she saw that all my incoming calls came from the same number. She just barked an order. "Put your friend on speaker and pretend you're alone."

"She only speaks Italian."

"*Non c'è problema*," she said in a thick Teutonic accent. Her demand had all the trappings of non-negotiability.

If Angela Marino betrayed her identity I'd have to eliminate this broad in front of me, but I couldn't ignore the fact that she hadn't come alone, that her little friend was waiting outside, ready to barge in.

I nodded gravely. More Vaseline to show her that I understood their need to take precautions. I called the cop, casting an eye around the place for an object with which to bludgeon Balakian's drudge.

"Now what is it?" answered Marino, arrogant, brusque as ever.

Not the best foot to start off on. "*Scusa, amore*," I began. "I know I shouldn't have called but I wanted to tell you that I love you, that I love you so much, and I'm afraid that destiny will divide us forever."

Silence. Marino wasn't so clever after all. I turned to the woman and smiled, ready to grab a chair and break it over her head. I was calculating the distance when I heard my "sweetheart" speak up.

"Oh, Attilio," she managed between sobs. "We can't afford to be afraid right now. I love you too. And all I want is to spend the rest of our new lives together."

Oscar-worthy performance. I peeped the woman. She was calm.

"Sorry for before but I was feeling a little down and needed reassurance."

"I'm glad you called, Attilio. But you have to be careful. My husband is very suspicious."

I mumbled a goodbye and hung up. I lowered my gaze to affect deep feelings.

"What's her name?"

"I'll happily tell you everything once we start getting serious."

She looked me over, searching for cracks that could tip her off to any possible lies. Then she got up, put on her jacket, took from her purse a pair of gloves lined with deer fur, and slowly put them on.

"In the event that we show up, Mr. Sforza."

"In the event? What's that mean?"

"That there will be no more meets arranged. If we choose to proceed we know where to find you. Always."

She'd been perfectly clear. I wouldn't be able to evade their surveillance, which had already gone on for a good bit. These guys were the best; you didn't bullshit Balakian. That explained why the big brains at special ops had lost two agents.

I pulled back the curtain and watched the woman walk off. Only then did I notice she had a strange gait, though I was sure it was a little show put on in my honor. She knew my eyes were glued to her bony ass and she was having fun fucking with me.

Across the street, in plain view on the sidewalk, her partner was looking at me with a smirk on his lips. Maybe he liked me.

I had to contact Marino. We were in trouble and needed to plug any holes before they found out that the woman I'd sworn my love to was a cop.

I couldn't discount their having bugged the house. But going out meant I'd be seen on the phone, and this time I couldn't get by with just a couple of sweet nothings. I opened the door and climbed the stairs to the roof. I was greeted by a freezing wind, took shelter behind a small structure, and pulled out my cellphone.

"What happened?" she asked anxiously.

"Close call," I replied. I was careful not leave anything out about the woman's visit. "They'll be checking the number and expecting a name and story," I said.

Marino sighed. "I'm on it. But it'll take time."

"You've underestimated them once again," I shouted. I was fed up. "The problem is you're no match for them, and I don't want to get killed. At this point I see no harm in parting ways."

"Pellegrini?"

"What?"

"You work for me, you're my puppet, and I'm the one pulling the strings," she said calmly. "Just try worming your way out of this and I'll devote every minute of my life to hunting you down and making you pay."

"I'm no use to you dead or locked up."

"You're useful to me alive and free, and we'll protect you. Now keep it together and wait for my next instructions."

I returned to the apartment and made coffee. The situation I found myself in was a mess. I was at the mercy of Balakian and Marino, with nothing to do and no way to act. This had never happened to me before. I'd always been master of my own affairs.

I needed to think, to find an alternative. I'd always found a way to turn the tables to my advantage, but this time I'd been caught off guard. I bundled up and went out. Night had fallen, and out of the corner of my eye I saw a shadow step out of a parked car and gently close the door.

I started walking slowly toward the subway stop.

FOUR

Vienna was buried under a scrim of dark rainclouds. We'd traveled all night trying to sleep in the bunks on the EuroNight, which made its final stop at Central Station.

While we stood in an orderly line to get a taxi, I lit my first cigarette and called Campagna.

"We'll be gone awhile."

"That sounds like good news to me," he replied. "The Dottoressa and her boys left yesterday. All of a sudden and without saying a word, no surprise."

"Any bright ideas?"

"There must have been a screwup. Something major. They were acting nervous, the way cops get when a case goes south."

"Maybe Pellegrini got himself in trouble."

"Maybe."

"There's nothing you can do?"

"I could, but I don't see any reason to."

I hung up. Some fucking cop.

Rossini and I made eye contact.

"Campagna?" he asked.

"Angela Marino left the city."

"Let's hope she's not headed to Vienna," grumbled the Fat Man.

It was possible, but I wouldn't bet on it. It made sense to think that Pellegrini had moved on. Otherwise Slezak's widow would have found him a long time ago.

Our taxi driver was an old pro. When he realized our destination was a luxury hotel, he pulled out all the stops to earn a good tip. In a mix of languages, he rattled off a litany of useful addresses for three men on their own. When he asked us what line of work we were in, Max, drowsy and on edge after skipping breakfast, grumbled, "Extermination." For his bad joke we were treated to a tutorial on Vienna's rats.

The hotel bar where Pierino Martinenghi worked was packed with a cheerful, rowdy party of Koreans. So, on his recommendation, we crossed the street and entered a bakery.

The Fat Man was tempted to argue with the waiter about why they didn't serve Sachertorte. He couldn't believe that he'd happened into the one place in Vienna that didn't carry it on the menu, but he perked up upon discovering that the mother of the owner was originally from Graz and made fried Krapfen following—to the letter—a seventeenth-century recipe.

He mumbled with his mouth full: "Delicious, lubricious, mind-blowing."

"Great," I snapped, "you finally made your peace with the world. Till two minutes ago you were impossible."

He shrugged. "I know. But you don't have to bitch about it like we're an old married couple."

Beniamino shook his head in amazement. "Some things I just don't want to hear. I'm going to see about Pierino," he muttered on his way out.

I brooded on the Fat Man's words. "Worrisome, don't you think?"

He smiled. "Nothing that can't be resolved with a good Krapfen," he said, thrusting the plate of sweets my way.

I bit into one, hoping it would have a therapeutic effect. It really was delicious. Max neatly wiped his mouth. I had known him for so long that I could tell he was about to launch into a lengthy disquisition about our relationship.

I didn't want to get sucked into idle talk. I summed things up before he could open his mouth: "We've lived together for too many years and need stable relationships with women who love us. Period."

He waved his chubby hand. "Right, more or less," he stammered, disappointed.

A few minutes later Rossini came back with Pierino in tow. They called Pierino the Punisher, because once he had made up his mind, he wouldn't quit until he'd cracked the safe. By the end of the '80s, his stubbornness had landed him in jail.

"That one was playing hard to get. Didn't want to give up the goods. I never even realized it was morning." He loved to recall his misadventure. The mark was the payroll of a big engineering company around Lodigiano, before the factories were relocated east. The Conforti in the boss's office had resisted his overtures, and at eight in the morning Pierino found himself surrounded by employees, who handed him over to the *carabinieri*.

Being locked up forced him to reflect on his profession, and he decided to change his methods, wise up, and, above all, study. He'd never give up safes—what in the good old days the Roman mob called 'widows'—and he understood that security technology is an enemy that only knowledge can defeat.

So the Punisher boned up, and now he was moving from one wealthy European country to another, planning each hit with the scrupulousness he needed to guarantee he could pull it off and not get arrested again.

He worked reception in hotels, got by admirably in several foreign languages, knew his trade. More importantly, he was a really likeable guy. Everyone liked him. In the field he was known for his honesty. He maintained good relationships with various criminal outfits that might turn out useful for him. About his personal life we didn't know much. Pierino jealously guarded his private affairs. Never talked about them. A sign of great intelligence and professionalism.

He limited himself to a handshake; kissing ex-cons on the cheek wouldn't have gone unnoticed. "Good to see you, boys," he said softly.

Underneath his heavy herringbone coat he wore a modest brown suit and a white tie that bore the hotel logo.

"Pierino's short on time," said Rossini. "He's got to get back to work."

"We have several departures this morning and I handle the bills," he explained. "But you can count on me for anything. I already found you a safe place to stay for at least three weeks. It'll cost you three hundred a day."

He removed a set of keys from his pants pocket and wrote the address on a napkin. His handwriting was crystal clear. He must have been the teacher's pet at grade school; in our day, they paid attention to those kinds of details.

"How else can I help?" he asked impatiently.

"We want to meet Paz Anaya Vega," I replied.

Martinenghi looked stunned. "Tobias Slezak's widow?"

"Exactly," said Max.

The Punisher had principles and, like us, considered drugs out of the question.

"What the hell do you guys have to do with that drug-trafficking ring?"

Old Rossini placed a hand on his shoulder. "Nothing," he said bluntly. "I can't say anything more about it."

Pierino stood up. "Slezak's men run the cocaine racket at the hotels. I know them, but with a request like that, I need to give them something."

"You're free to tell them that we have information about the man in Padua," I said. "It's the truth. And if you vouch for our seriousness, I don't foresee any problems."

"All right."

Pretending to pay the bill, Martinenghi reached into his pocket and placed a cell phone on the table, which disappeared inside Max's jacket. "Make sure it's always on," he instructed.

We ordered another round of coffee.

"We did well going to Pierino," said the Fat Man, satisfied. "He's all right."

"Old guard," Rossini said with pride. "On their way to extinction, but a couple of them are left."

I peeped what the safecracker had written on the napkin.

"Do we have any idea where Oswaldgasse in Altmannsdorf is?"

"No," replied Max, taking the tablet out of his bag. "But we'll soon find out."

"Check out how to reach the area by public transit," added Beniamino. "The time has come to move with a minimum of caution."

The neighborhood was in Meidling, Vienna's twelfth district. The apartment was on the second floor of a building mostly inhabited by young couples, close to stores and bars that we'd never set foot in. No point in drawing attention to yourself around your hideout.

Entrance, living room, kitchen, three bedrooms, two toilets, and a balcony equipped with a capacious ashtray. A handwritten sign informed us smoking was prohibited. No doubt we'd break that rule. We'd make amends with a bottle of the good stuff and a card.

We picked our rooms and unpacked the few things we'd brought with us. We didn't have the slightest idea how long we'd be staying in Austria, but traveling light was imperative. Anything else we could pick up in loco.

I stretched out on the bed and caught up on a little sleep, skipping lunch. I still hadn't digested the Krapfen I'd polished off.

Midafternoon I took a shower and shaved. The store-bought shaving cream and disposable razor gave me no satisfaction. Once again it dawned on me that the time to shave was in the morning, soon as you're up, when your skin's refreshed. I'd read it on a blog where shaving fanatics bandied about different schools of thought.

The house was empty. My friends had gone out, but in the kitchen I discovered they'd already taken care of the shopping. I snacked on crackers and an Austrian version of Liptauer. The abundance of cumin muffled the taste of sheep's-milk cheese. Sort of. To tell the truth, it wasn't necessarily a bad thing. I'd never been a gourmet. I washed down this latest dilemma with a couple of glasses of Riesling. I smoked and watched a heavy mix of rain and snow fall and melt the minute it hit the ground.

After a while I grew tired. It was one of those days I didn't even want to think. Or listen to music. I would have gone back to bed and woken up the following morning after a deep, dreamless sleep, but a phone rang. The ringtone was an hysterical version of a well-known polka the name of which I couldn't remember. "Rosamunde" maybe. I listened to the jingle and spotted the source on the table in the entrance. It was the phone Martinenghi gave us.

"I spoke to those people," he said. "They seemed interested. The meet is tonight, 10 P.M., at a hotel bar near the Schottenring station."

"We'll be there."

"Not all three of you," he clarified. "The deal was one person from each party."

"I'll go."

"I figured."

"You know the place?"

"I'm the one who chose it. It's packed with high rollers, and management is very discreet."

I was surprised. I'd been expecting a long, unsettling wait, and instead they'd agreed to meet us right away.

They took Pierino at his word. And the chance to get information about Slezak's killer must have thrilled them.

A little later my partners returned. They'd gone to get a car. Our trusted car smuggler, Dario Tomasella, knew a guy in Lienz who had a cousin in Vienna—

I cut short Rossini's story with a wave of my hand. There's nothing more tedious and complicated than the web of who-knows-who in the crime world. "Did you find one?"

Beniamino looked at Max and smiled. "You'll be pleased to hear we have a Škoda."

"A Superb, not a Felicia, the latest model," said the Fat Man.

"Clean?" I asked.

"Not exactly," replied the Old Gangster. "We parked it in a garage not too close, but at least we have a vehicle ready in case of emergencies. Tomorrow morning I have a meeting with a guy to get a couple of pistols."

"I already aired my disapproval," Max interrupted. "What if they were already used for dirty work?"

"Gun prices in Vienna are outrageous," objected Rossini. "Besides, I doubt we'll need them. Plus we're short on money."

I turned to the Fat Man; he handled the purse strings. "How much is left?"

He cleared his throat. "27,800 euros. Plus change."

"What?" I shouted. "This shit is costing us a fortune."

"It's been a bit since we've had revenue," observed Beniamino. "Pretty soon I'll have to pull a heist so we're not forced to beg."

I peeped the clock and switched the subject. "In a couple hours I'm meeting a member of Paz Anaya Vega's organization."

"Then you better rehearse your lines before you go on," advised the Fat Man.

The hotel was housed inside a majestic nineteenth-century building. The pomp and circumstance of imperial Vienna remained visible despite a few obvious modern upgrades to the building's structure and design. The whole Central European arrangement was tasteful. The bar was particularly inviting, the music just the right volume for savoring a drop in blessed peace. It was a joint for real drinkers. Solitaries too. My kind of place. The kind where everybody can safely assume that behind people's thirst there's serious, complicated, painful business going on, which a drink can make more tolerable. And no one dares pass judgment.

I breathed in the air and caught the scent of spiced tobacco; someone here was a fan of the legendary Balkan Sobranie. Thick white columns of smoke rose from the middle of the room where a man with a pipe sat. I remembered then that in Austria the smoking prohibition had been put off for another couple of years, but I'd left my pack in my coat pocket. I may be an inveterate smoker but abusing tobacco is my choice. Anyone who works in bars has the right to not breathe my smoke. Alcohol would do me.

The two barmen weren't green; they knew their trade. I sat down on a high stool at the bar and pointed to a bottle of Calvados Roger Groult, which came served in the proper glass—a real rarity. I shook my head firmly when the other bartender tried to talk me into pairing my nectar with dark chocolate from Tuscany, just as a celebrity chef had suggested on TV.

It wasn't the finest chocolate, sure, but more to the point, apple brandy's got nothing to do with cacao. Max was right: In the name of taste people had lost their minds and the world was now full of bullshit gurus steering the market. They tout the highest standards and then make a killing advertising products for the most toxic food industries.

Fortunately the Roger Groult didn't disappoint. I sucked it

down and asked the bartender to top me off. I had time. I'd arrived a good half hour early.

The envoy of the outfit turned up on time. I spotted him a mile away: sixty-five-ish, past exploits with biker gangs written all over him. Tall, burly, he was dressed head to toe in dark leather. Handlebar moustache. Apart from his bald crown, he had shoulder-length hair, which he dyed brick red in an effort to recapture a color that had faded a long time ago.

I'd been expecting someone less conspicuous but noticed that no one took much interest in him.

He sat down at an empty table and ordered a beer. I walked over and took the seat across from him.

"I'm Marco," I said, introducing myself in English and extending a hand.

"You can call me Abo," he said in decent Italian, inflected with a dialect that I couldn't quite pin down.

He could tell I was curious. "I served five years in the tank at Ascoli Piceno," he explained with a frown.

"One of the less welcoming," I remarked.

"I don't have fond memories of Italy."

The same bartender who had served me brought him a vodka tonic.

"Thanks for taking this meeting," I said out of respect for good manners.

Abo appreciated it. "We're willing to pay large for information on the guy . . . as long as we're talking about the same person."

"Giorgio Pellegrini."

"That's him, the very same piece of shit."

It pleased me to find that Handsome Giorgio made friends wherever he went. "We're not selling information," I clarified. "We want to propose teaming up to locate and eliminate him."

He took a drink and dipped his fat finger in a bowl of

cashews. "We might be interested, but I'd have to talk with my bosses. They only sent me because I speak your language."

He was lying. They'd never have sent an errand boy. Our man had to be able to check the quality of what we were offering. And to do that, he needed to know every last detail of the score.

Obviously I played along. I laid an ace on the table so that he understood we were serious. "Pellegrini's working for the cops. He's at the center of a major undercover operation run by the Italian Ministry of the Interior."

The Austrian blanched at this bit of news. It meant not only did they risk losing a boss and two affiliates, but that the Italian police could provide their Austrian counterparts with proof of the crew's criminal activity. Pellegrini's testimony would be the killshot.

"You sure?" he asked anxiously.

"Positive."

"What else do you know?"

"Your turn."

He nodded. "Pellegrini shows up in Vienna out of the blue, calling himself Attilio Sforza," he began. "He puts the word out that he's looking to score a big batch of coke. Because one of our old clients said he knew him well, we took it into consideration. We turned it inside out, but his story held up. Now I know why: he had the Italian police behind him."

"Your client really played you for suckers."

"Once we found him he confessed it was Interpol that forced him to vouch for Sforza."

"And he didn't testify against you?"

"No. We didn't eliminate him either. There's dirt on him only we know about, and he can't afford for it to be aired in a courtroom."

Must've been hell, I thought, being double-blackmailed by people who were fighting an all-out war, but I wasn't there to make small talk.

"Ultimately Tobias decided to close the deal, but Pellegrini tricked him and killed him and two other comrades," he said, almost choking up. "One was my son-in-law Guntmar. Left my daughter Sabine all alone with two little kids."

He raised his glass. I half-heartedly raised my own. "To Guntmar," he said softly.

After a long swig, he was ready to go on.

"Pellegrini ran off with the money but left four kilos of quality coke. His one objective was to murder Tobias. We ran a probe to figure out whether he had backers or was acting out a personal vendetta, but until today all we'd managed to discover was his true identity."

"How'd you do that?"

He shrugged. "We contacted one of the many companies in Moscow that traffic in the world of 'communications.' Two days later we knew all about Pellegrini. We won't make the same mistake twice. Next time we'll go straight to the Russians."

"We'll give you our coordinates to make the job easier," I said, as if it were the norm. In truth, I was fed up. I didn't like the idea of Russian hackers sticking their noses into our lives, our business. You couldn't trust them. There was no way of foreseeing how they'd use the information. In just a few years they'd become so effective, so brazen as to interfere in the elections of the most powerful country on earth.

He smiled. "We've already made inquiries based on what Martinenghi gave us."

"Seems fair," I let slip.

Abo ordered another round and politely bid me to continue our exchange of information. The time had come to furnish him with the worst news. I took out my phone and showed the Austrian the photo of Paz Anaya Vega taken at La Nena.

"We know it was you who butchered the wife and lover. Martina and Gemma were their names, and they didn't deserve that horrible end," I said sternly.

The man didn't blink. His eyes, however, gleamed with satisfaction. I knew then that he'd been there that night in Padua to avenge his son-in-law. Once again I cursed Giorgio Pellegrini for forcing me to mix with people this repugnant.

"The Italian police are also in possession of the photo. It was taken by one of Pellegrini's accomplices," I added, exhibiting the same cool. "There's probably a warrant out on Paz already. In Italy that amounts to a life sentence."

Abo was shaken. Now there were no lingering doubts that their organization would be wiped out by a joint Austrian-Italian operation.

I twisted the knife. "You went to all that trouble proving you were a big-time operation, and then the Spaniard gets made at the scene of the crime. You slaughtered two unarmed women and now you've been had. Maybe you're not so clever after all."

"Then why did you come looking for us?"

"Thanks to Pellegrini we're looking at jail time too," I replied. "The only way out of this for both of us is to kill him."

He drained his glass and grunted: "I'll let you know." He was in a hurry to get out of there, tell the others what he'd just learned, and take action to salvage what was left to salvage.

But I wasn't done. "Next time I want to meet Paz Anaya Vega. And I want you to tell her we don't take kindly to drug traffickers and we don't kill innocent bystanders."

He grabbed me by the collar of my coat. "You're getting on my nerves," he spat, brandishing his left fist. On his middle and ring fingers he wore large rings topped with roughly cut rhinestones. Deadly weapons in the hands of a street fighter.

I looked around us. "We're in the bar of a luxury hotel," I reminded him.

He regained his composure, and I made myself even more explicit. "If Paz wants a deal, she's got to keep in mind that pointless killings won't be tolerated."

Abo stood up. He took a few bills out of his wallet and tossed them on the table: "We'll get in touch through Martinenghi." He walked off with his head down, like a bull about to charge.

Had we brokered an alliance, things would have still turned out badly. We had no intention of forgetting the murders of Martina and Gemma.

I wouldn't have made our feelings so obvious on the first meeting, but Old Rossini was adamant: respect the rules, whatever the cost. If you have to strike a deal with an enemy, you better make it clear your principles are legit and always will be.

Rules. No one respects them anymore. They're so far removed from the new criminal mindset that it's become difficult to explain them. Insisting they be respected in good faith is out of the question; inevitably, you have to flex your muscles.

I finished my third Calvados. If I wanted to have a fourth or fifth and still return home with my dignity intact, I'd have to take precautions. The bartender sensed this immediately and rushed to bring me a bottle of water and a club sandwich.

A classic remedy, obviously, the best thing to prepare one's stomach for another drink: three wedges of white bread, crisp bacon, a slice of turkey, tomato, lettuce, and condiments. I added a shot of Tabasco—my personal touch.

It was at that moment I saw a woman enter and head over to the bar. I still didn't know that my life would change, and I was more interested in my stomach than in her. I watched her chat with the bartender then turn to have a look around the room. I could tell immediately that she was a working girl scoping the place for clients. I carried on eating, thinking about Abo, Paz, and Pellegrini. She had the bartender pour two fingers of amber liquor that I couldn't identify and went back to looking at the men sitting alone.

She had three options: yours truly, the gentleman with the pipe, and another guy, probably American, wearing a Pork Pie hat that barely rested on his ash-colored moptop and drinking a Bloody Mary.

I wagered she'd make her way to my table. Instead she set her sights on the guy with the hat, but after a minute he began apologizing and gesticulating wildly. He wanted to be left alone.

The woman looked in my direction, and, as a courtesy, I invited her to join my table.

"My name's Edith," she said, still on her feet. "And you?"

Her English was uninflected, and a cone of shadow made it impossible for me to make her out. "Marco," I replied. "Why don't you take a seat?"

"Because you're eating to keep from getting drunk."

"So?"

"Men are a drag in general, but when they drink they get violent. They insult you or hurt you and then blame it on booze."

That was the truth, and it was pointless to swear that I was different, that she wasn't running any risks with me. She didn't know me, and I didn't want to sleep with her anyways.

"So your only other option is the gentleman with the pipe."

"I know him," she said. "He comes here once a month and sits there drinking and smoking while he waits on a lady. They always get the same room. 309. I've been in it and I don't see what's so special."

"I guess it'll remain a mystery."

She shrugged and gave a sigh of disappointment while checking out the clientele again.

"How much do you charge?"

"Depends. Anyway, I don't have any intention of going with you."

"Me neither. But I'm tired of staring up at you. I'm getting a cramp in my neck. If your price isn't too high, I'll pay you for the company."

She pulled up a chair. "I'm not that desperate yet," she said, a little hurt. "I can drink with whomever I want without charging a 'price.'"

"I didn't mean to offend you," I hastened to say.

"I don't like the word 'price.' Never liked it," she said. "It's off-putting."

"I apologize," I said again. I was beginning to realize that maybe she was worth taking a look at.

Blonde, blue-eyed, her full lips fire red. She was real pretty. She must have just turned forty. She had on a snug jacket that showed off her ample cleavage. She reminded me of someone, and when I leaned over the edge of the table to get a look at her legs, it became clear who.

"What's with you?" she snapped. "I don't like being looked at like that. You're a real pig. Italians usually have better manners."

I put up my arms. "I humbly beg your pardon. It's just I haven't seen a replica of Tempest Storm this perfect in a while," I explained admiringly. "You're something special, Edith."

She relaxed, and for the first time let me get a glimpse of her smile. "I see you know what you're talking about."

The blues are to blame. Once, looking for a version of Allison Heartington's "Blues Heart" on YouTube, I came across a video from 1955 featuring a B-list burlesque star whose stage name was Tempest Storm.

I've never been a fan of burlesque, but I've always liked busty pin-ups and seductive stars in classic movies.

"Now I'm curious to see what you're really like."

"What do you mean?"

I brushed the sleeve of her jacket. "You're faking. You're reciting a script. I want to meet you when you're not working."

She smiled again. "I thought you wanted to see me naked."

"I admit I wouldn't mind."

"But first you want to see the normal version. You're a one-step-at-a-time kind of guy."

"Not always."

She patted her blonde hair. "I'm a brunette."

"I imagined."

"Now I'm blonde. Everywhere."

"I imagined that too."

"You imagine a lot of things."

"It happens when I meet a girl I like."

"And I like being called a girl."

"Can we see each other again?"

She hesitated.

"I'm not a john," I said firmly. "I wouldn't break any rules that didn't need breaking."

"People think girls like me are alone in the world and readily available," she said. "But I could have a man, children, relatives, a dog, two cats. A life all my own."

"You could. And I still wouldn't want any part of it," I repeated. "All I want is to know the other Edith."

"Who said the real one is worth knowing."

"I'll be the one to decide."

She leaned in and put her mouth to my ear. "Clients follow a script too," she whispered, sending a shiver up my spine. "You really think getting to know one another would do either of us any good?"

I was relishing the moment. "Your questions are too complicated, and I don't know how to answer them. But the way you ask is delicious."

She laughed and stood up. "Sometimes, around eleven, I go have breakfast at Jonas Reindl Coffee on Währinger Straße," she said. "I might just be there tomorrow."

"And I might just pass by."

I kept my eyes on her ass as she left. I was intrigued, even if

I'd used her presence to get shed of the disgust I felt after having had to interact with the deplorable likes of Abo.

I signaled the bartender to bring me the check. As I was paying I inquired about Edith.

"Nice, right? I've known her since I started working here," he said. "She's one of Frau Vieira's girls."

I was caught off guard. Prostitution is legal, regulated, and taxed in Austria.

"I thought she worked out of pocket."

His tone changed. "Here in Vienna only repped whores set foot in luxury hotels."

'Repped.' I turned the word over. Funny way of saying exploited by a madam.

I took out the phone Martinenghi gave me and called him.

"Trouble?" he asked in a sleepy voice.

"Sorry, Pierino, I'm just calling about a personal matter. What can you tell me about Frau Vieira?"

"A fucking madam?" he said, irritated. "You woke me up to ask about hookers in Vienna?"

"Just Frau Vieira."

"Can't we talk about this tomorrow?"

"Now is better."

He sighed. "She's an old Portuguese harpy. Arrived in Vienna thirty years ago. Got her start streetwalking in Prater before establishing a sophisticated organization backed by the cops."

"I thought pimping was obsolete under the new law."

"Only in legit brothels," he explained, "but hookers mainly work outside in designated areas. There are only two in Vienna, and protection has become necessary, not so much for their safety but to keep the women in check. The majority come from the East believing they'll find a job and instead wind up on the street."

The same old story. "Thanks for the information, Pierino."

"I don't know how it's of help, but I recommend you give Frau Vieira a wide berth."

"Why's that?"

"She's deceitful, perverse, cruel," he replied, drawing out each word. "And her men, all Portuguese like her, are dangerous. Everyone who underestimated them, who thought they were dealing with the usual pimps that only asserted themselves with women, was forced to think again."

"The guy I met tonight, Paz Anaya Vega's envoy, had all the makings of a real mean son of a bitch too."

"He tell you his name?"

"Said his name was Abo. Big man with a handlebar moustache."

"Abo Tscherne. Back in the day he was mixed up with the Hells Angels. Later he did business with Tobias Slezak," he explained. "Now he's the number two. After Paz."

"He acted as if he was an errand boy sent by the bosses just because he spoke Italian."

Pierino chuckled, amused. "The guy wants to take the Spaniard's place. Claims it's his right. But some of the crew disagrees."

"Why's that?"

"Turns out he doesn't have the brains for business. His role has always been to keep the street in check by breaking their competitors' bones."

He'd wanted to have his fun with me too.

It had stopped raining. The temperature had dropped. Despite the late hour, a few taxis idled in front of the hotel. I climbed into the one at the head of the line, driven by a Serb, and had him drop me off a few hundred yards from our apartment. Beniamino had advised us to take the most basic precautions. All I was adopting was a pale imitation of them, but I was tired and didn't want to play hide-and-seek with a couple of tails through half of Vienna in the cold. I slipped into an entrance hall and smoked a whole cigarette while checking for anyone who looked suspicious. The street was desolate, empty.

My friends were waiting for me in the living room, smoking and drinking. Grappa for Max, vodka for Rossini. The bottle of Calvados was still sealed. They hadn't forgotten. Kindnesses among people who care about one another. What greeted me across the doorstep was real warmth. Details, I thought, are what make the difference in people's lives. Solitude can be unrelenting sometimes; it had always scared me more than death itself.

As my time on earth slipped by, I increasingly felt the need to wake up with someone by my side. More and more often I opened my eyes and reached out to touch a face, a hand. A desire to love, to be loved.

Then there's friendship. Which is a complicated, messy business. But its returns are priceless.

I gave a detailed account of my meeting with the envoy from Paz Anaya Vega's outfit. "I'm convinced that they'll break off communications," I said in the end.

"What makes you think that?" asked the Fat Man.

"They know the police will make mincemeat of them. It's just a question of time," I answered, pouring myself just a splash of Calvados. I'd already had enough to drink that night. "The one shot they have at surviving is to bolt to another continent."

"The only one capable of going underground is Paz," Old Rossini broke in. "She's already done it and I'm sure she has a plan to avoid prison. But nothing's going to stop her from getting revenge. The reason she killed Pellegrini's women was to signal loud and clear that he'd meet the same end."

Max pointed at Rossini. "I agree with Beniamino. The Spaniard is clever, but now there's just one thing on her mind: skinning Giorgio. That's why she'll team up with us."

"And you think she'll stop at him?" I added, mulling over the declaration of war I'd dished to Abo Tscherne.

"At this point there's a line of people waiting to eliminate us," the Fat Man replied, resigned. "What's one more?"

Beniamino put out his cigarette. "I'm going to sleep."

"Excellent idea," said Max, following suit.

"What's the rush?" I protested. "I haven't finished my story."

"What else happened?"

"I met a girl."

The Fat Man sat back down, and Rossini leaned forward to get a better look at me. "So that's what took you so long."

"Out with it," exhorted the other.

I didn't need coaxing. And I didn't leave out what Pierino Martinenghi had told me.

"Obviously you're planning to go to that café tomorrow in the hopes of running into her," Max said to change the subject.

"Obviously."

Beniamino rested his hand on the Fat Man's shoulder.

"Did you see the look on Marco's face? Haven't we seen that look before?" he asked. "Tomorrow he'll be back to sing us the same old song."

Max stood and began crooning an old Gino Paoli hit. Rossini joined in for the chorus:

Non ci sarà un altro amore
non ci sarà un'altra volta
non ho più il cuore libero
non c'è spazio per altre storie

"That never happened!" I cried, scandalized. But I knew I was lying, so I poured another round and stoically faced the memory of some entanglements about which I'd spent words of a certain gravity only to regret them bitterly shortly afterward.

"Well," yawned Old Rossini a little later, "remember to bring the phone in the off chance Abo or Paz and their little pals get in touch."

Jonas Reindl Coffee was a shrewd operation that married high-end design and quality coffee. Vienna had long been the European capital of the drink. A group of importers, roasters, and shops had staked their money on a superior range of products. After all, the first shop to serve coffee was opened in the Austrian capital right after the expulsion of the Ottomans, who had laid siege to the city for a long time. In the enemy camps they'd found sacks filled with dark beans. A Pole who'd lived in Turkey came up with the idea to sell cups of them. In Italy coffee made its first appearance in Venice around 1570, imported by a botanist from Padua.

I knew the whole history of coffee. It was the thesis subject of a student who had lost her head for yours truly. She was a real beauty, and I'd wanted to sleep with her, but I couldn't get over the age difference. She pursued me for a couple months, and I got her to talk about her research in order to stave off subjects that I wouldn't know how to negotiate intelligently. Then I backed off. I didn't want to run the risk of alcohol drowning out the last vestiges of prudence and steering me straight into her bed.

As usual, I was early. I ordered a cappuccino and a slice of cake and took a seat at a table. While I tucked into my breakfast I scanned the clientele. This didn't seem like a place Edith would normally frequent. There were several tourists, and the other patrons looked like they were just passing through. To my right a middle-aged couple was engrossed in their reading. She a book, he *Der Standard*. Their leather briefcases and formal attire gave the impression that they were professionals on break, lawyers maybe. Were I in Italy I wouldn't have wavered—by then I could identify them at a glance. A little later three Italian women came in. As soon as they sat down they began talking about the city, like dutiful tourists. Judging from their accents they were from Puglia. They described a Vienna I'd never know, since beautiful places and fine art weren't on my criminal itinerary. Luckier people find nourishment in beauty and culture. It's a form of resisting the prevailing squalor. One necessary for bearing the idea that this world won't ever get better, according to Max. I shielded myself with the blues but knew it wasn't enough. Beauty and crime are incompatible, even if you're one of the good guys, even if your intention is to set things straight, right some wrong.

In any case, I was intrigued, and I followed their talk with interest. Listening to them plan their vacation was pleasant. Then they started taking selfies to post to their Facebook profiles—another fundamental custom of the modern world that we were excluded from.

Suddenly I realized that Edith had arrived and was having fun scrutinizing me.

"Do you like them?" she asked in English, pointing to the tourists. "I don't see a pretty girl among them."

"I was envying their lightheartedness."

"Do you always have deep thoughts first thing in the morning?"

I didn't answer. I was too busy drinking her in. Aside from the color of her hair, which she now wore in a ponytail, she was a completely different woman from the one I'd met in the hotel bar.

Her thick, Tempest Storm makeup had hid her delicately featured face. Her dark green eyes stood out against her pale skin. Her lips were full, yes, but more beautiful without lipstick.

When she removed her coat I let my eyes scroll down her soft curves, no longer hemmed in by her pin-up dress.

"You're beautiful," I whispered.

She pretended not to hear and held out her hand.

"My name is Edith Amaral."

"Marco Buratti, pleased to meet you."

She glanced at the menu. "I'll have a caffè moka and a crois-sant."

I stood up, got in line at the cash register, and approached the counter—all without taking my eyes off her. I really liked her. I felt lucky to have met her. And I was ready to court her. Common sense told me to let it go, a fling was the last thing to pursue given the danger I was in.

But the odds of meeting another woman like her were as good as the odds of escaping Pellegrini and Dottoressa Marino's trap unscathed. By the time I got back to the table with her tray I'd dismissed any doubts. But it wouldn't take much to ruin the whole thing. Which is exactly what happened when I asked, given her last name, whether she was Austrian.

"I've lived in Vienna for over twenty years. But I was born in Portugal. My mother was Dutch and my father came from the District of Leiria."

"Frau Vieira is Portuguese too," I said, regretting the words the very next moment.

Edith stiffened. "How did you come to be so well informed?"

"I asked around."

"Why? It's not normal for some guy you meet in a bar to want to know certain things." She was furious. And anxious too.

I'm not just some guy was the best answer that came to mind.

"What's that mean?"

I'd backed myself into a corner. "I know how the world works, I'm well acquainted with certain scenes."

"Either you're a cop or a felon."

"I'm neither," I replied, embarrassed. "It's hard to explain."

It was probably my attitude and fuzzy explanations that led her to believe that Frau Vieira herself had sent me.

"She paid you to test me, is that it?" she asked, tears in her eyes.

"No," I said, taking her hand. "I don't know her. It's just a name I heard. Bar talk, nothing more."

She wasn't buying it. She wriggled out of my grasp. Panic had taken hold of her. "I can't take this anymore," she stammered. "Tell her, I'm begging you. I ran off one time and I didn't even like the guy. I've been good. I've taken on another persona just as she wanted. I still turn a good profit. Okay, I'm not young anymore and I don't turn heads the way I once did, but I can count on a good group of johns in their fifties. She knows that. I'll pay back everything I owe."

"Knock it off," I snapped. It hurt to listen to her.

But she carried on. She lowered her voice to an incomprehensible murmur then shot to her feet. "I'm still her old whore. She can trust me," she said before snatching up her jacket and purse and running out.

The three Italians and the other customers looked on, baffled. I was sure they hadn't understood a word of our conversation and that to them the scene they'd just witnessed was nothing more than a lover's quarrel. In which I'd come off looking like the typical male asshole. And I was, in part.

I decided to follow her, but as soon as I stepped outside I realized it was useless. I didn't know which way she'd gone and she was already too far away to pick out of the crowd of pedestrians on the sidewalk.

I was upset. I kept asking myself how the hell I'd allowed myself to act that way. I'd managed to thread pearls of stupidity in almost scientific fashion. Once I calmed down I began to brood on Edith's reaction. She was terrified and, as far as I could tell, she had unsuccessfully attempted to escape mistreatment at the hands of Frau Vieira before. She'd paid dearly for that rash decision.

Edith had referred to herself as an "old whore," an appellative typically reserved for prostitutes who prospered in their prime and later, to remain marketable, zeroed in on clients of a certain age. And tastes. That's why that night she'd transformed herself into a copy—prettier for that matter—of Tempest Storm.

I needed someone to talk to but my partners had an appointment with a guy about a gun. I wandered aimlessly in the cold then gave up and went for a beer. All I could think about was Edith, and when the phone that Martinenghi had given me rang, I struggled to snap out of it.

"Paz Anaya Vega has agreed to meet you and proposes tomorrow night at Sopron," said Pierino.

"Where?"

"Just across the Hungarian border, about fifty miles from Vienna."

So the Spaniard was hiding out in Hungary, within arm's reach. I was tempted to accept but the safecracker came to my rescue.

"The wine is good, especially the Kékfrankos. Blaufränkisch, the Austrians call it. If you prefer red wine—"

"Well?"

"I wouldn't trust it," he spoke up. "Lately there's a chill in the air around those parts, and the local police is a lot more trigger happy around foreigners. Paz on the other hand, she's at home there. You catch my drift?"

"Perfectly. Any place in Vienna you'd recommend?"

"The hotel bar is safe. Anybody could slip in and out unnoticed. Even Paz."

There was a chance of running into Edith there, and being in the company of a drug-dealer wouldn't look good, but I couldn't complain to Pierino.

I called Rossini, who asked me to meet them in a restaurant on Naglergasse, in the old part of town. Upon entering I immediately spotted Max working his way through a gigantic steak with roast potatoes and onions. He was too busy stuffing his face to do more than nod.

"There was no use arguing," sighed Beniamino, picking at a salad. "Max insisted on eating here. He claims it's one of the last traditional restaurants in the city. If you ask me, it looks full of American tourists."

The Fat Man caught his breath, took a swig of beer, and defended his decision. I ordered a dish at random and asked about their meeting that morning.

"Two old cannons from the Eastern bloc," said Rossini. "They cost us fifty euro a day."

The price had really dropped. "They must be junk."

"Let's pray we don't need to use them."

I told them about Martinenghi's phone call. Clumped along. I wanted to get around to talking about Edith.

"The Spaniard wanted to lure you to some out-of-the-way nook and subject you to one of her special treatments to get you to talk," said Beniamino. "The woman is cold all right. But I don't understand how she could think we'd walk into a trap that obvious."

"To be honest, I almost fell for it," I mumbled, embarrassed. "I wasn't thinking straight."

Max and Rossini elbowed each other. "This girl's got you off balance."

"No, the truth is I'm a real asshole."

"What the hell happened?" asked Beniamino. "She sent you packing on the first date?"

"Worse," I spoke up. "I scared her off."

I told them what happened. My friends remained silent, grim-faced. Old Rossini especially. Like us, he hated pimps, only in his case he'd often shown it the hard way. He once went to war with a group of Albanian mobsters who'd kidnapped a group of young women, turned them into sex slaves, and eventually brought them to the province of Treviso. He helped a few escape and then the situation took a turn for the worse. A Greek girl, fearing they'd attack her family in retaliation, made the mistake of going back to her captors. To set an example, they murdered her, and two days later Beniamino threw the guy responsible into the river.

The real problem is, in the age of globalization, prostitution is an unstoppable phenomenon: human beings worth something on the sex market, especially women and children, are transformed into goods, for sale or rent. Exploited until they die. Supply is overwhelming but doesn't meet demand, and demand appears to be bottomless.

Beniamino ran a hand over his face. "You can't help them all, but if you find one who's in real trouble, you can't just look the other way either, right?"

Right. That was our fate. And that principle didn't only apply to prostitutes. Whenever we came across a sad story, we tried to give it a dignified ending.

"Unfortunately, first we have to save ourselves before we can be of use to Edith," he went on. "But in the meantime, we can try to find out more about her case."

"Frau Vieira," Max uttered with disdain. "Sounds like a kapo name."

I was relieved. And grateful. And proud that we were willing to go for broke for a woman only one of us had met at a bar, since, as Beniamino said, you can't always stand on the sidelines and watch. Outlaw hearts.

Martinenghi called a little after 8 P.M. Max had shut himself up in the kitchen and was attempting to make a traditional local soup with liver dumplings. The smell was not tantalizing, and Old Rossini and I withdrew to the living room with a bottle of chilled Grüner Veltliner.

"These pistols aren't as bad as I thought," he said, staring down one of the barrels against the light. The rest was dismantled and waiting to be cleaned. "They can come in handy close-up, thirty feet at best. The caliber's nothing special, and the bullets were made in Yugolavia, back when it was still a country."

"Even if they were brand new they wouldn't be much use against Paz's men. They're roughnecks on their own turf."

Rossini touched his chest. "Our army is all here. You do what you can and maybe for once luck will be on our side."

Just then the cellphone's polka ringtone broke in. I hit speaker.

"They've agreed," said the safecracker. "Paz is expecting you at the hotel bar in three hours sharp."

"Thanks, Pierino."

"I can promise the place is safe but I can't speak for their intentions," he added gravely.

"I'll be careful," I reassured him, before switching the subject. "Sorry to impose on you again, but I need some information about a woman who works for Frau Vieira."

"What's her name?"

"Edith Amaral."

"Don't know her. She doesn't hustle in my hotel. I can ask one of the girls I'm on good terms with," he said. Then, after a long pause, he added, "But if my friend doesn't know anything or doesn't want to talk, my hands are tied."

"If it's going to create problems for you, don't worry about it."

"I'm in no position to meddle with these people, I'm sorry," he explained, getting worked up. "I'd be on shaky ground and they'd start asking too many questions. Not to mention break a bone or two."

"I get it. Find out what you can without running any risks."

"I'll be in touch."

I looked at Rossini.

"Paz won't come alone," he said. "Her men will be planted in the right places. There's no saying they won't try to snatch you at the end of the meeting."

I felt a shiver down my spine. "And where will you be?"

The Old Gangster pointed at the dismantled pistol. "Sprawled out in the hall, packing this hardware in my coat pockets. We go in together and we go out together. Max'll be hiding in the neighborhood, ready with the car."

"Sounds like the perfect plan," I joked.

"Pierino will do what he can and that's already a lot," added Rossini. "Where a pimp's involved, the cops are right around the corner. If he blows his cover, he won't be able to crack safes anymore."

"I know. I hate to stir up trouble for him, but I don't know who else to turn to in Vienna."

"We've gotten people in fixes in the past because we put our needs above theirs."

"What does that mean?"

"That Pierino's one of us."

An outlaw of the old guard. I knew.

"We'll take precautions, play it safe," I promised, though I understood what he'd meant. I said 'we,' but I was the one who had to be careful not to overstep my bounds. My friend was right to warn me; I've been known to get my priorities mixed up.

Beniamino poured more wine and changed the subject. "Let's hope Max is whipping up a light dinner—we don't have much time to digest."

"Wishful thinking," I answered.

The liver dumplings dropped like stones in our stomachs, but we didn't mention it. We were nervous and disinclined to joke around. When the Fat Man asked our opinion out loud, I managed to steer a middle course. On the whole the meal was good, I swore. But he wasn't convinced.

"You sound like an old Christian Democrat," he said, not even looking up from his plate. He meant it as a slight.

It came time for us to leave. Rossini put on a double-breasted pinstripe suit and a white scarf. Underneath his camel hair jacket the ensemble was the epitome of cool. Vienna seemed colder than usual. The winter was implacable, wouldn't let up.

We climbed into the Superb and reached the hotel's neighborhood. Max went looking for a parking spot close enough to pick us up in a matter of seconds.

Beniamino and I continued on foot. We didn't notice anything suspicious. In the hall we found two mugs sitting on a couch. Their attempts to appear indifferent tipped us off. Rossini took a seat right in front of them, his hands planted in his pockets.

Abo, seated at the bar, paid the bill the moment he saw me and slipped out a back door that led to the old gaming room. As far as I'd gleaned from Pierino, the room was now reserved for reading and chess.

The bartender recognized me and led me to the same table from the evening before. He'd come to know that drinkers are creatures of habit. He brought me a Calvados before I'd even ordered one. He deserved a good tip.

I'd had a few sips when Paz made her entrance. I recognized her immediately; she was exactly the same as in the photos Zorzi had taken in Padua. I waved discreetly to get her attention, but it was beside the point: she was heading my way.

She had on a low-necked dress, short and snug. Were circumstances different I'd have said she wanted to catch my eye. And she would have succeeded, no sweat—she was a knockout. A bombshell, to use the scientific classification of my saxophonist friend Maurizio Camardi. I couldn't help but muse over the fact that the vile women in this whole affair, Angela Marino and the Spaniard, were to die for. Straight out of a film from the '40s.

"I'll speak Castilian and you speak Italian. We'll understand one another perfectly," she said without preamble while placing a handbag roomy enough for a "lady's gun" on the table. Some brands had launched lines of brightly colored bags, or bags adorned with gold inserts, but they weren't her style.

"What are you drinking?" I asked.

"Nothing. I imagine you won't take offense, will you?"

Another wicked witch, I thought. Her attitude was aggressive, totally unfriendly. She and Marino had something besides beauty in common.

"You're right, my offer was too polite for a drug dealer who assaults, tortures, and murders defenseless women."

Her pretty lips formed a scowl.

"Abo said you were a shmuck. He wasn't off the mark."

"If it weren't for this shmuck, you'd still be unwise to the fact that your organization is fucked and you're looking at life behind bars."

"I'm the type that lands on her feet."

"Giorgio Pellegrini once told me the very same thing."

Her expression changed. She was the picture of hatred itself.

"Do you know where he is?"

"No."

"Then what good are you to me?"

"I may know a way to get to that piece of shit. You on the other hand, you don't even know where to begin."

"How did you make me?"

"Italian police."

"The Austrian cops on my payroll say their Italian colleagues haven't contacted them yet."

"It's early. In the meantime they're blackmailing us to keep you far from Pellegrini."

"In what way?"

"Certainly not by sharing a table like this."

"From what we hear you guys are a couple cards short of a deck," she said. "You're a failed singer, your friend in the hall is a retired smuggler, and the one waiting in the car is an obese terrorist."

"Your Russian hackers aren't up to speed. I hope you didn't pay them too much."

She shrugged. "You're non-entities. But sometimes losers come to know things of interest. That's the only reason I accepted your invitation. But no way are we going to work together."

"So what's your offer then?"

"You tell me where I can find Tobias' murderer, I kill him, and with him dead, you avoid jail."

"Finding him is exactly why we have to join forces," I explained matter-of-factly. "Pellegrini is involved in a secret operation with the Italian police, and that means he's not holed up somewhere. On the contrary, he's trying to infiltrate an organization, if he hasn't succeeded in doing so already. Exactly like he did with you."

"You think we haven't already tapped all of our contacts to figure out what happened to him? There's a million-dollar bounty on his head, but no one's come forward yet."

"That's not the way to hunt him down."

"What does that mean?"

"Why did he kill your man?"

"It's a mystery," she replied, a mix of rage, incredulity, and sadness. "He came to Vienna under a false name just to kill Tobias while closing a deal. He could have shot him any time. Instead he put together a warped plan and ran unnecessary risks."

"Would you like to know what this short deck thinks?"

"That's why I'm here," she said with an extra pinch of sarcasm.

For a minute I thought about walking away. But I took

another sip and cooled down. I had to bite my tongue if I was to dispense with both her and Pellegrini. Martina and Gemma deserved justice, and we were the only ones who cared to serve it.

"Well then?"

"Pellegrini murdered Slezak to attract attention," I said, choosing my words carefully to drive home the point. "He was after the credentials that he needed to enter into contact with another criminal organization—the real target of the operation."

The Spaniard's attitude changed. Now she was listening.

"If what you claim is true, that means that the order to kill my husband came from the Italian police."

"Not necessarily. It may have been Pellegrini's idea. Of course, someone allowed it to go down."

"And do you know the names of those responsible?"

"Yes," I replied. "I know what's running through your mind and the answer is no. We won't let you retaliate against Italian cops. You've already murdered innocent people."

"Those cops aren't innocent."

"No, but Pellegrini is the only one who deserves to die."

"So says you."

"By that logic, I think that you ought to pay with your life too. Yet here we are, looking for a solution to our problem, which is and remains eliminating Giorgio Pellegrini."

She crossed her legs and stared at me in silence. Then she called the bartender over and ordered a glass of Lustau, a 30-year-old Spanish sherry that costs an eyeball. My empty glass was filled with another generous pour of Calvados.

"Which were you sleeping with, the wife or the other one?" She didn't give me time to respond. "The friend was fat and ugly, but she held out longer. She was used to pain, familiar with violence, knew how to take it."

"I'm not listening."

"So it was her."

"Her name is Gemma and that's all that need concern you."

"As long as you're not looking to avenge her death."

For a moment I felt like explaining to her the difference between justice and vengeance. To show her that my idea of justice didn't involve cops and courts. But my mind was racing with images of the restaurant cellar, blood, mutilated bodies, and I decided not to. She wouldn't have understood, and besides, some subjects are best avoided when you're with enemies.

"One thing at a time," I said. "Let's take care of Pellegrini first."

She sipped her sherry without averting her gaze. She knew she had a pair of eyes that could bring men to their knees, but I was immune because I hated her. Not her personally, but the category of despicable beings she belonged to. Drug dealers reek of death, sell death, use it to gain power and corner markets. They jockey to see who can be cruelest. They get famous and then die like animals.

"What can I do besides double the bounty?"

Ah, finally, Paz had deigned to hear me out. Now was my chance and I couldn't blow it.

"Withdraw it," I said, "it won't help. I already told you, not only is Pellegrini not in hiding, he's also hard at work trying to make contact with another organization."

"So?" she pressed on.

"Your organization is confined to drug dealers. That's not enough. You have to enter into contact with other sorts of criminals."

She clenched an expletive between her teeth. "And how do I do that? Put an ad out in the paper?"

"In a manner of speaking," I answered, pausing to take a drink. "Pay your Russian hackers to get the word out to people who matter. They know who. Pellegrini isn't a ghost. You can get them to pass around his photo, spread the rumor that he probably still goes by the name Attilio Sforza. Whoever gets the message will pass it on to the next guy."

"I have to admit, I let myself get played, and that'll damage my good name and my business."

"Do you really think your outfit will survive?"

"No, but that's exactly why I have to consider the future."

"You can't turn the page until after you've avenged the death of your man Tobias."

She made a show of putting her hand to her heart.

"You're so right, I forgot I was a poor inconsolable widow."

I'd asked for it. A cloying appeal to her feelings was a misstep.

"I'll take your advice," she said, picking up her purse.

She was about to leave but changed her mind.

"You're a real strange crew: you play multiple tables at a time, have a direct line to the cops who killed Tobias, and, despite counting for shit, you have the balls to let me know I deserve to die," she whispered. "I should kill you just for being an anomaly. But if I find Pellegrini, I'll let it go."

Before I could respond, I caught the guile in her eyes. We'd sidestepped the trap she'd set for us in Sopron, but she had no intention of forgetting about us. For all the reasons she'd just listed.

Paz Anaya Vega was all pride and power on her way out. And I breathed a sigh of relief. I couldn't wait to step outside and have a smoke. I asked for the check, but the bartender told me not to worry, the woman had a running tab at the hotel. I left a large tip anyway. On my way to the coat check I ran into Edith. She was leaning against a wall, the amber glow from a lampshade lit her face, now pinched, glaring, disgusted. She'd seen me with Paz Anaya Vega and now she was sure that I was a dangerous, evil man.

I would have gone to her to assuage her feelings but I was

afraid I was being watched and walked on past. With a heavy heart.

Beniamino stood up as soon as he saw me. He flashed a smile at the two assholes and followed me out. Max pulled up, and we drove off after checking to make sure we weren't being followed.

"So?" asked the Fat Man. "Anyone want to tell me what happened?"

"You should have seen how she looked at me. Repulsed."

"Who, the Spaniard?"

"No. Edith."

Old Rossini, sitting in back, reached out and squeezed my shoulder. "Now's not the time, Marco," he said coolly. "We can talk about it at the house, but now you've got to focus. Call the cop."

I pulled out the phone that I used to communicate with Campagna. To snap out of it, I lit a cigarette and smoked half.

"I don't suffer from insomnia and now that I'm cashing checks for nothing I go to bed without a care," the inspector started yakking.

"We found Paz Anaya Vega," I cut in.

"Where?"

"In Vienna."

"So that's where you've been holed up. Marino will be glad to know you didn't change your identity and flee the continent. She calls me every day asking for news."

"She's not back in Padua?"

"No. And I can't say I miss her."

"Tell her for the moment she doesn't need to fear for Pellegrini's life," I lied. "The Spaniard has more pressing issues to resolve."

"What does that mean?"

"An old lieutenant of the dearly departed Tobias Slezak wants to take her out, and Paz isn't at liberty to leave the city."

"Anything else?"

"Yeah. We've done what we were blackmailed to do," I said. "Now it's Marino's turn to keep up her end of the bargain. We're through with her fucking schemes."

"I'll pass it on. But if I were you I'd be in no rush to get back home," he said before hanging up.

We weren't that stupid. We would stay and watch. And in the meantime we'd take care of Edith.

Paz was right: we were playing multiple tables at a time.

FIVE

I went on the lam three days and three nights. I switched off the cellphone that I used to communicate with Dottoressa Marino and lost Serj Balakian's men. After recouping my fake documents and money, which I'd had the foresight to stash in a locker at the train station upon arriving in Munich, I checked into a room at a shoddy B&B near Dachau. Then I returned to Munich by train and hunted for a safe place to hide if things went south.

But that wasn't my only reason. I needed to pry loose from that claustrophobic situation, where I was under surveillance day and night. I know myself too well. I can't handle psychological stress for long. Plus I wanted to send a message to beautiful, know-it-all Angela Marino, who took a free and easy attitude toward an informer like me. Last, I had to teach Balakian's skinny bitch a thing or two about life; she presumed to give me lessons on behaving like a fugitive—a way of convincing her boss that the time had come to quit with the foreplay and meet face to face. Then I'd have his ass. I couldn't wait to get back to my life as a respectable, hardworking, and honest citizen of the Italian Republic.

Survival is a subject I could teach at the best colleges. The only way to hide in a large European city with a good degree of safety and elude high-class criminal organizations on your tail and cops armed with sophisticated means was to fly under the radar. Don't use IDs, ATMs, credit cards, cellphones. Don't sleep at hotels, rent apartments, or buy or lease cars.

And don't surf the Internet. I had to turn the clock back twenty years.

The best safehouse is a room to rent in a private home. But not just any home. Avoid families and couples like the plague. Look for single women in their fifties and sixties. After two mornings and two afternoons I'd zeroed in on five, but only one, Toska Köhler, had passed the first tests.

A widow for six years, retired one. Her closest relatives lived hundreds of miles away. The minute I entered her house I saw signs of loneliness and resignation in her face. It was clear she'd expected more from life and couldn't figure out why that hadn't come to pass. Her decision to rent a room in her apartment wasn't a matter of money but a practical means of breaking up the monotony and warding off ghosts that can complicate one's ability to carry on. I made an appearance of being polite, courteous, and a touch indecisive. I told her I came from Lugano and was looking for a place to stay in the city while I pursued my sommelier business, the one profession I could credibly lay claim to thanks to my lengthy tenure at La Nena. I got her talking about regional wine and gauged how pliable she was. She proved to be a malleable subject.

I acted hard to please about the room: the furniture arrangement wouldn't do, the TV wasn't up to my standards. She was accommodating about every last detail. She didn't want me going elsewhere.

She had raved about the neighborhood in the online ad I'd found: "Scwabing-West: young, quiet, safe."

When she served me crap coffee with some simple honey and cinnamon cookies that she'd made with her own little hands, I administered the killshot: I asked her if there were any movie theaters or playhouses in the area. She lit up. She pictured the two of us going together!

Rent was seven hundred euro. I paid for the first three months in cash, slept there the first night, and told her I'd be back soon. We could work out the details then, I added. She didn't bat an eye.

I was handsome, charming, elegant. I looked respectable. Toska was already at my feet. She would put me up for as long as I needed, and I would exceed her wildest expectations. All of them. Her life would no longer be governed by a flat, gray, dreary ordinariness. If she survived, she'd never forget me.

The productive break had done me good. When I opened the door to the apartment in Neuperlach, I was back to the old Giorgio Pellegrini. I curled my lip to find that the place had been ransacked, and this time they hadn't worried about covering their tracks. Balakian must have beaten the guys tailing me for having lost me in an underground parking lot, and they had taken their revenge by throwing coffee and sugar all over the floor.

The minute I turned my phone back on I heard a long series of beeps. My "sweetheart" had written me earnest messages begging me to contact her, saying she couldn't live without me. Marino outdid herself. She'd managed to bury her unprecedented anger under a mountain of mawkishness.

"*Ciao, amore mio.*"

"I'm so happy to hear your voice," she chirped. "I was worried about you. How are you?"

"Fine."

"I arrived in Munich yesterday."

"Imagine that!" I cried, pretending to be happy.

"We have to see each other. I'm at Saint Michael's Church. You know he's my favorite saint."

I didn't doubt it; he was the patron saint of cops, after all. But translating her code for emergencies, the message meant something else entirely. I had to head out to a spot in Sophienstraße.

Thirty minutes later I was ready to play cat-and-mouse with Balakian's men, standing in Marienplatz, where the usual throngs of tourists were milling about. I cut west in the direction of Saint Michael's Church, but at Neuhauserstraße I pulled a rabbit out of my hat and literally vanished into thin air. By a long, circuitous route I arrived in Karsplatz and crossed the Alter Botanischer Garten. Sergeant Marmorato was there to make sure no one was shadowing me. A few minutes later, I entered the Park Café.

I recognized another cop, Pitta, pretending to check his phone by the entrance. Angela Marino was waiting for me at a table in a far corner to the right of the large lunch counter.

As I approached I realized that I'd been a naughty boy for running off. The haggard look on her face, the baggy eyes, the pale lips—clearly she'd been through hell. Which was understandable, after all: the outcome of an important sting operation depends entirely on one man, and should he decide to duck out right in the middle of things, it could blow someone's career.

I didn't stand on ceremony or mince words: "Don't start busting my balls with your threats. I've shown you I could care less."

"So I'm to assume that this getaway wasn't just some bumbling fuck up but meant to teach me a lesson," she replied ironically.

"Exactly."

She crossed her hands under her chin. Another pose in her repertoire. She didn't wear rings and her pale pink nail polish was in urgent need of repair. Personally, I'd have replaced it with a bolder color.

"I'm listening, Giorgio."

"I want to know the whole truth about this operation and most of all I want guarantees."

"Did I hear you right? Did you say 'guarantees'?"

She couldn't help it. Spite was her forte.

"I realized a long time ago that you had it in for me. But if you want to play out this scene with Balakian, we have to set straight how I walk away with immunity."

"We've been over this before."

"All I heard were vague promises that reeked of a raw deal. I want all the details or I'm not moving a finger until I'm in possession of a document signed by a judge, preferably a federal judge. You get the point: someone heavy."

She shook her head and looked at me as if she were an adult who couldn't get through to a teenage boy.

"You know it doesn't work that way," she began. "In our country you don't get immunity the way you do in the United States. You'll have to submit to being placed under arrest, confess, and testify at trial. Then you'll be set free, and we'll provide you with a new identity."

Then you'll be set free. That's where the raw deal lay hidden. Not only was she unsure when that would happen, but another charge would be enough to keep me locked up for who knows how long.

"I've already been an informant once."

"I'm well aware."

"And I have no intention of playing that role again and rotting in a cell."

At that point her expression changed. She was losing her patience but had to hear me out. She couldn't afford my standing up and taking another vacation. Maybe a longer one.

She needed a break to simmer down, and when a waiter passed by, she seized the chance to order. She settled on a salad and beer. I on the other hand was hungry and opted for pork ribs and potatoes with sour cream. Our drinks arrived immediately, and Angela ignored me when I gestured to toast glasses.

"Honestly I don't understand why, at a moment as delicate as this, we have to return to arguing about trivial details like the trial."

"Because you still don't get that you'll have to do it without me."

"We need a witness who can draw the connection between Paz Anaya Vega and the accused—Buratti, Rossini, Max the Memory, and Campagna," she insisted, "and make them accessories to the murder of your wife and girlfriend *and* drug trafficking. At the opportune time they'll be caught in possession of three kilos of cocaine."

"I can do you one better," I snapped. "I can attest to having seen that relic Rossini shoot to kill. I can nail the cop who covered it all up. I'd be more than happy to repay those dicks the favor after they forced me out of Padua. But I'll only show up in court footloose and with immunity in my pocket."

"I want to be honest," said Marino. "At the moment I can't guarantee anything. To give you what you're asking I need time to get various people to come to an agreement. I can promise you, however, that I will do everything possible if you'll go back to being operative."

"How can I refuse in the face of such honesty?" I replied sarcastically.

"Now's the time to button things up with Balakian," she went on. "Buratti and his partners have found out that Paz Anaya Vega is back in Vienna and has put her hunt on pause for the time being, because someone else is hard up for the little queen's drug-trafficking throne."

Bravo, *tres amigos*. Swept up by their moral outrage to exact justice for Gemma and Martina, they had finally found the Spaniard. Three dipshits from the provinces, willingly walking into court to be slaughtered by yours truly.

"When are you planning on putting them back behind bars?"

"What I hear from Inspector Campagna, they should be in Padua in a few days. We'll give them time to be seen around town, then narcotics will be tipped off."

I wondered if Buratti and his partners were all that stupid.

"It doesn't strike you as being a little too easy?"

Angela Marino held out her arms. "So what if it is? What chance do they stand against the law, which has finally decided to give them their just deserts? Their fate is sealed no matter what."

I enjoyed baiting her.

"When all's said and done, I deserve a long sentence too."

"You're different, Giorgio," she replied with suspicious alacrity, as if she'd been waiting for the chance to rub my nose in the harsh truth. "You're an almost perfect criminal machine. Your whole life you've had the wisdom to align yourself with those in a position of greater power, and that makes you useful to us. You have been in the past, you are now, and you always will be."

I saw what she was driving at.

"I'm particularly adept at doing the dirty work."

Angela Marino nodded, gauging my reaction. But I didn't take offense that easy. Instead I was sorry I couldn't show her, not then and not ever, that serving the powers that be gave me the chance to create an empire all my own, where I was free to be me and could get my needs met. All the more so since I have always had a great gift: knowing how to content myself.

"Buratti and his friends are more of a threat than you," the cop continued. "They assume the right to defy the state in the name of storybook principles. In this big arena, they always take the side of the bull. They're useless has-beens and have to be eliminated because they're unshakeable. Or so they think. I'm going to have fun pitting them against one another and watching them jockey to take the stand."

I began to seriously question whether Marino was not a little disturbed. If that was her idea of fun, there was nothing to be happy about.

"Tell me about the operation," I asked, picking a rib clean. The ribs at La Nena were light years better.

"First I have to bring you up to speed," she answered, a strange flicker in her eyes. "We gave some thought to that business with your phone call, when you convinced Balakian's men that you were in a relationship with a woman."

"They came this close to catching me," I remarked.

"Well, that woman's in Munich now and won't leave your side again."

"Is that right?" I teased. "And who is she?"

"It's me, dear," she gushed. "I'll be spending every waking moment with you, and if you try to pull another stunt, I'll kill you."

Cheap shot. This would complicate everything.

"You're not up to it," I objected. "You've got cop written all over you. These guys are professionals, and someone like you, who's always hid behind the safety of her uniform and rank, two bites and they'll devour you. Let me handle the dirty work. I'll be just fine on my own."

She angrily speared a slice of pepper. "Shut your hole," she hissed. "No one asked for your opinion and no one wants to hear it."

"Then explain this: why have I been here in plain view to build trust with this crew just to start all over again from scratch?"

"Because it's easier if two of us bring an end to this operation. We believe they're more likely to trust a couple. Besides, it gives us an opportunity to justify your disappearance."

"I ran to come get you."

"Exactly."

"Do you have an identity that'll pass inspection?"

"Made in record time after that woman listened in on our sweet talk."

"Will it stand scrutiny?"

"They've already stuck their noses in it. Our experts have picked up their digital footprint. They know the woman you love is called Daniela Sileo." She stood up. "We're going home," she ordered.

I stayed put. "We're not going anywhere until you start talking about this fucking operation."

She leaned over and took my face in her hands.

"I give the orders, honey, and don't you ever forget it," she whispered. "Now peel your pretty tush off the chair and come with me. I'll tell you everything outside."

I gave in. She was no walk in the park, but having her close might be to my advantage.

We headed toward San Michele, where we expected to be spotted and tailed by Balakian's men. Marmorato and Pitta followed at a distance. When we got to the church we didn't notice anybody, not even on our way to Neuperlach. Balakian had called off his scouts.

Marino blamed me. "You slipped out of sight and they've decided not to trust you," she kept repeating. She made me long for Martina and Gemma. One look and they'd shut up, whereas this broad didn't know her place.

I was sure there was another reason for Balakian's indifference, even if I couldn't figure out what it was. I hazarded a guess.

"If Paz Anaya Vega managed to discover my name isn't Attilio Sforza but Giorgio Pellegrini, maybe they figured it out too."

She dismissed the thought with a nervous wave of her hand. "We created your cover down to the last detail, and the Spaniard moves in circles that have no points of contact with Balakian's organization."

"Then the problem is you," I pointed out in the futile hope she'd get lost.

"Tomorrow morning you'll contact the intermediary, break the news about me, and return to following procedure."

Yessir, you bitch, I thought as she threaded her arm in mine. We looked like a couple whispering sweet nothings, when in fact Angela Marino had finally decided to tell me the truth.

When she was through, I pointed out that we both stood to gain a lot if we pulled off the operation successfully. She a big promotion, me immunity for life.

No one knew if Serj Balakian actually existed or if he was an artfully assembled myth. What was undeniable was that the organization had been operating for at least twenty years and offered a truly unique—and therefore highly expensive—service: it created new lives. Just like any federal witness protection program, they provided identities, places of residence, professions, and more, depending on the needs of their clients.

The difference between their outfit and government agencies was that they didn't protect good people but criminals who had chosen to cut ties with their past, their accomplices, their "families"—people who could afford it.

I was enthralled. The idea was pure genius, but in order to work it relied on the help of corrupt cops and officials in several countries. In the halls of Interpol word had it that the organization was led by their colleagues. Italian investigators suspected that the program had been developed inside structures created by various governments to handle ex-war criminals, terrorists, and high-ranking officials from Iraq, Libya, Syria, and any other shithole that had something the world powers were itching to get their hands on. A hodgepodge of collaborators, informers, relatives, lovers, and witnesses who had to be relocated elsewhere.

And they made a fuss about granting me immunity!

"If the press got its hands on a story like that, people wouldn't look at you the same way."

After a huff of disappointment, the cop seized on the opportunity to launch another pointless salvo.

"Buratti and his friends would never have made a comment like that. They understand that there are levels of vice that the media is incapable of confronting. Even for quote-unquote public opinion, that's a step too far."

Hot air disguised as a higher order of rationale.

"You're no saint either," I retorted, riled. "I didn't see you all shook up when you ordered me to kill those fools in Vienna."

She stopped and looked me dead in the eye. I should have kept my mouth shut; when certain things spill out just because you have your nuts in a knot, you're immediately labeled unreliable. A threat. Someone they'd be better off eliminating if they really wanted to feel at ease.

I lowered my gaze so that she knew I knew that I'd acted like an idiot, and she went back to walking and talking as if nothing had happened.

"You're right, I'm no saint, but the situation is so compromised that we can't afford not to get our hands dirty. Besides, us non-saints are what people like you need. Without me you'd already be serving life."

The operation assigned to Marino by the heavies at the Ministry of the Interior was seriously dirty: infiltrating a new "client" with the aim of identifying several of the outfit's members, capturing them, then forcing them to say where they'd hid a guy who'd gone on the lam.

"So, who's the target of the operation?"

"His name's not important. But we're counting on him to transform the latest scandal into an historic occasion to clean up some circles that think they're untouchable."

"Sorry, but it sounds pretty slippery to me."

"All you need to know is that we're looking for someone, and in order to find him we have to tear down Balakian's organization. Be glad you know that much."

The Dottoressa had woken up early and gone to take a shower. Obviously, she'd slept in my bed, and I'd taken the most uncomfortable couch in all Munich. I wondered if she'd slept with one eye open, worried that I'd suddenly turn up with the worst intentions.

She entered the kitchen wrapped in a large towel. A smaller one covered her wet hair. I noticed that she had pretty feet and slender ankles adorned with gold chains. She went to the window and studied the street.

"Get up," she ordered. "We'll get breakfast and then go to the intermediary's."

I didn't say anything. I wanted her to turn around and look at me. When she did, I gave her one of my irresistible looks. She noticed but decided it was of no interest. I should have expected as much.

To spite her, I took my time. I jerked off slowly, fantasizing about Toska, my new landlady. I'd make her pay for the humiliation I'd suffered for too long at the hands of Dottoressa Marino. Between the two women, the differences in age and beauty were clear, but I could content myself.

It wasn't a particularly cold day. The uptick of two degrees made it pleasant to stroll the streets of that neighborhood, outlying yet dignified, like almost all of Munich. It's a city I could live in—middle class and attentive to decorum. But Italy is something else entirely.

Marino settled on a German chain store that served awful coffee. I made do with an anonymous brand of tea and a multigrain croissant. The Dottoressa ordered a cappuccino and toast with mixed-berry jam.

She was in a bad mood, absorbed in god knows what kind of super-cop thoughts. She didn't snap to until I informed her that Miss Bones had walked in. The woman placed her order at the counter and walked over to our table carrying a tray. Coffee, veal sausage, Bretzel, and orange juice.

She sat down, smiled, mumbled hello. Then she dug into her breakfast.

"May I introduce Ms. Daniela Sileo," I said, tetchy about the embarrassing situation that had cropped up.

"There's no need, I already know her," interrupted the woman in Italian. Her accent hurt my ears. "I'm only here to get some answers, Mr. Sforza."

"Shoot," I said, stealing a glance at Marino. All she had to do was keep her mouth shut this once.

"Why did you fall off our radar?"

"You want the truth?"

"Please."

"Because I had to retrieve Daniela in total safety, and to show you and your boss that I'm good, that if I want I can shake off the best of them."

She tightened her thin lips into a faint smile. Or was she frowning?

"You're a man who doesn't care for lectures. I get it. But in our book, that's not an admirable quality."

I leaped to correct her.

"All I wanted was to show you that I can adapt to your level of security. It won't happen again."

"Does Ms. Sileo want to use our services too?"

"Yes," I replied, flashing my sweetheart a smile.

"The price will increase considerably."

"How much are we talking?"

"Six million dollars."

I looked at Marino, who signaled her consent.

"Agreed," I answered.

"How long will it take to come up with the money?"

"A couple days."

The woman nodded, satisfied.

"You'll deliver it to Attorney Charents the day after tomorrow, at ten sharp, then we'll come collect you."

I'd been involved in crime too long to trust her.

"That seems unreasonable," I objected. "It seems fairer to me if we deposit half. The other half we'll give you once you've delivered us to safety."

"You have to follow our procedures to the letter," replied Miss Bones, sipping her coffee.

"There's just one hitch: you could change your mind and keep the money."

"Our service is based on trust," she pointed out, leaning toward me. "If you're not prepared to place blind trust in our resources, maybe we should reconsider our relationship."

I was about to respond when Marino delivered a sharp kick to my right shin.

"You're perfectly right," I hastened to say. "I just needed a little time to get used to the idea."

"Leaving behind the criminal mindset isn't easy for people like you, Mr. Sforza," continued the woman. "But you have to realize that we're the only ones who can offer you a shot at a new life with Ms. Sileo, an honest life. Once it's done, illegal behavior will not be tolerated."

"What does that mean?" I asked. "We never talked about that before."

"Because we had yet to decide whether or not to accept your candidacy. But now we need to be clear. The most important thing is that you are both aware that we cannot imperil our existence because of crimes our clients commit. Understood?"

"I'm not sure."

The woman had run out of patience. "And I thought I'd been clear: we physically remove anyone who gets out of line."

She turned to Marino. "Once you've dropped off the money, you must go back home and await our arrival. Don't move for any reason."

"Agreed," mumbled the cop.

The other woman stood up. While she was putting on her

long overcoat and adjusting her gray felt hat, I asked her if she knew our final destination.

"I don't know anything," she answered. "My colleagues and I only have to deliver you to another branch of our organization."

She nodded goodbye. "Till soon, messieurs," she said, a touch formal, then added: "There are better places to have breakfast in Munich."

We waited for her to leave before conferring.

"With that face, it shouldn't be hard to identify her," considered Marino, who was already planning our next move.

I shrugged. "What does it matter if we know the name of some gofer? If you want to find out where they've hidden the guy you're after, we have to piece together the whole organization. Which means we have to trust them to 'protect' us for god knows how long."

"If we want to stop the outfit from reorganizing in the future, we have to identify most of their affiliates anyways."

The cops can't abide the existence of a "company" that effective. Especially if its partners are hiding behind their uniforms.

"And the money?" I asked with a pinch of malice. "Where are you going to come up with six million dollars?"

"We're constantly sequestering piles of cash. You know that. And not all of it ends up on the books."

"The dirty war against crime comes at a price," I rejoined ironically.

She ignored me. She took her phone and exited the place. I watched her through the glass as she talked. Barked orders, more like it. She signaled me to join her.

"The money will be here tomorrow night along with a team of agents. Things are beginning to get serious."

"What are they coming for? Not to follow us, I hope. It won't take long for these guys to realize what's up."

"For now they'll stick to photographing the individuals that come to get us."

"Some comfort. Balakian's men are cops—or were cops. They know how to defend themselves."

"But our people are better. They won't be made."

Continuing the conversation was pointless. A waste of time.

"See you tomorrow night," I said, walking off.

She ran to catch up and grabbed my arm. "Where do you think you're going, sweetheart?"

"That's my fucking business," I said, wriggling free. "I don't have the slightest intention of having you around until we go see Attorney Charents."

"I think you better get used to the idea. I won't let you disappear again and jeopardize the entire operation."

I put my mouth to her ear. Her scent was intoxicating, and I whispered: "I need my space, understand? Otherwise I'll lose my mind and blow the whole thing up."

"If a whore is what you're after, a couple of hours should do you."

"No, I need a woman with strong moral fiber, someone irreproachable. I get off on leaving indelible memories, and whores don't have memories."

She looked at me in disgust. For the first time I'd managed to disturb her. The unflinching and incorruptible super-cop had seen an uncensored side of my personality and from then on she'd look at me different. For the worse, that much was clear, but at least I could be sure that she'd be more careful around me. She'd keep within her bounds and not push me, because I wasn't just some crook you could take for granted. I was hard to define, frightening.

"I could give a flying fuck about your needs," she said with swagger. "You're going to have to get used to my company."

I smiled. I wanted to see Toska Köhler but I knew that

Marino would have gone to great lengths to stop me. I felt better now, in any case. I could stand the wait.

We went back to the Park Café for lunch. The Dottoressa withdrew with Sergeant Marmorato for twenty minutes while the other cop, Pitta, kept an eye on me.

In the afternoon we went shopping at the supermarket near the house, like a regular couple.

"Get what you want," she said brusquely. "You owned a restaurant; you must know how to cook something."

The cop didn't know that I had once served a young woman trenette with pesto laced with aspirin. She too had decided to make things difficult for me. My guest was allergic, and the meal wasn't exactly to her liking.

Old times, other circumstances. Cooking had always been a pleasant way to pass the time, even if I didn't have a flair for it. I knew more about wine and liquor. I'm good at managing a restaurant, balancing the books, attracting clients, making them want to come back. Occasionally I argued over the menu with the chefs. Chefs think they're artists and believe people will order any dish they attach some extravagant name to. Some I fired, but more often than not we came to an agreement.

To feed the lady cop I zeroed in on a frozen rack of lamb from Scotland, which I roasted in the oven with spring onions, thyme, and lard, and paired with a 2011 Lemberger.

It turned out better than I'd expected, but the Dottoressa didn't have much of an appetite. She contented herself with a couple bites.

When she went off to bed I heard the distinct sound of a key turning in the lock and a chair being placed under the doorknob.

Small satisfactions while I awaited better days.

One million dollars in hundred-dollar bills weighs twenty

pounds. The problem was volume. We needed two large suit-cases, which were delivered to us the following evening in a hotel parking lot on the west side of town. We got there by taxi after an exhausting subway transfer and long stretches on foot. Marmorato and Pitta were like two retrievers—they kept trail-ing behind then running ahead to sniff out possible suspects.

By a stroke of luck, we seemed to have lost Balakian's men at Harras Station. We managed to board the train just before the doors closed. Out of the corner of my eye I thought I saw a guy in a dark wool hat, who hadn't made it on board, staring intensely in our direction. Just my impression. When you know you're being tailed, it feels like everyone is following you.

A couple of thirty-year-olds climbed out of a black station wagon parked in a dark corner. The woman was thickset but surprisingly nimble. The man, on the other hand, was tall and high ranking. Two operatives from the team that the ministry had sent to Munich at the behest of the pretty Dottoressa. They removed the suitcases from the trunk and handed them to us without saying a word.

We carried the bags to reception and asked them to do us the courtesy of calling a taxi. There was no need to play hide and seek. On the contrary, we wanted them to see us enter the house with the money.

An hour later I was seated on the couch, curiously examin-ing the two large suitcases. I was tempted to ask Marino to let me see the bills, all identical, all neatly wrapped in convenient stacks of ten-thousand dollars, but I was sure that she'd deny me the pleasure.

She noticed my interest.

"Obviously there are tracking devices inside and they've already been activated."

Obviously. It was a terrible idea.

"If they find them, we're dead."

"That won't happen. They won't find out."

I had ideas of my own about how to pull one over the next guy, but at the moment I wasn't the one giving orders. "Anyway, despite what it might look like, I'm not interested in the money," I pointed out. "I want to get back to my old life. Open another restaurant, rest on my laurels, amuse myself with a mistress, make friends in the right circles."

"And where do you think you'll set up shop this time?"

"Parma, Lucca, Piacenza," I fired off at random.

In reality I had long ago settled on Treviso, the perfect city for a boy of my talent and dedication. Even better than Padua. Plus, with Buratti and his partners keeping Campagna company in prison, I'd have nothing to fear.

The Dottoressa snatched up one of the suitcases and carried it into the bedroom. Less than a minute later, she hauled off the second one too.

Wise woman. She knew the old adage: "Opportunity makes the thief."

A little later, exiting the bathroom, I thought I heard a voice. I removed my shoes, tiptoed to the door, and put my ear against the thin wood.

Marino was whispering on her phone. I couldn't make out more than a handful of words, but her tone gave her away: there was a man in her life. I pictured a cop, older, higher ranking. She must have been attracted to older men, otherwise she'd never have resisted my charms. Sleeping with her would have been a real coup, would have saved me a lot of frustration, but I had to resign myself to the fact that my life had never been easy. I'd always had to take my due by force.

The next morning the cop had the nerve to wake me up at an ungodly hour.

"Piss off," I protested. "Our appointment with the attorney is at ten."

"We have to go over the plan and review every little detail," she replied. "We can't afford to make mistakes."

Another waste of time. I had the Dottoressa all figured out: she was a capable organizer with a maniacal predisposition, but she was slow to improvise. And experience had taught me that when you play dirty you have to be quick on your feet.

She didn't shut up until we were loading the suitcases in the taxi.

Sipan Charents had an office in Türkenstraße, on the fourth and top floor of a building not far from a famous pastry shop, where I planned on having breakfast as soon as we dropped off the money.

I'd only met the lawyer once, right after I'd killed Tobias Slezak and his two sidekicks. Marino had given me his name and address. He was a little elderly man with a full head of white hair. He wore ridiculous round eyeglasses with thick black frames. I set five thousand euros in cash on his desk, and he'd thanked me and asked me to explain my case. He listened to me very carefully and then said, in a thin little voice and fluent English, that he found my story interesting, that he wasn't sure he could be of help because he didn't know Serj Balakian, but that he would ask around.

He nodded goodbye, and his secretary, not much younger than him, escorted me to the door.

I had been in plenty of law offices before and the thing that had struck me most about his was the near total absence of case files. Even his legal codes and updates were scant and dated. Clearly Sipan Charents didn't take on new cases. He must have had a handful of carefully vetted, affluent clients.

Maybe he himself was Serj Balakian. I began to suspect as much when, instead of the secretary, Miss Bones greeted us.

She led us as far as the room where the lawyer asked us to

take a seat. Over his shoulder, leaning idly against the wall, was a muscular forty-something with the sleeves of his white shirt rolled to the elbow. His face, marked by barely visible scars at the arches of his eyebrows, indicated that he came from a line of boxers who had never won the kind of title that makes you famous. He wore baggy flannel pants held up by a pair of red suspenders. The word "gorilla" was tattooed across his fore-head.

"We have to check and count the money," said the elderly lawyer. He sounded in a hurry.

The woman unzipped both suitcases and, with the help of the gorilla, emptied the contents on the floor. Wrapped in sev-eral layers of clear plastic, the stacks of bills fell noiselessly on the thick Persian rug.

Then they carried the suitcases out and came back with a bill counter. Not just any bill counter. I'd once seen a similar model at a casino. It could count up to 1,500 bills a minute and discard any counterfeits.

No one breathed during the count. It worked out to the sum agreed upon, except there were four fake hundred-dollar bills.

The woman handed them back. "I'm guessing you only have euros on you."

I couldn't believe my ears. Six million dollars gently laid at their feet and this dim-bulb expected every last penny.

I took out my wallet, luckily full of cash despite my not hav-ing a debit or credit card, and made up the difference.

Attorney Charents stood up. "Thanks for your patience," he said and walked over to shake my hand and kiss Marino's. "Good luck," he added with a certain zeal.

On our way out, I saw the gorilla exit another room carry-ing two suitcases. Only not the ones we'd used to transport the money. Different brand, different color. Things were taking a turn for the worse. Those genius cops hadn't taken into account that Balakian's men might think to check for tracking devices or other electronic contraptions. If they found them, and I had little doubt that they would, we were in deep shit. They'd eliminate us before we'd reached our destination.

As soon as we stepped into the elevator I let the Dottoressa have it. She blanched.

"We can't go forward with the operation," she mumbled, visibly upset. "We have to call in the team to identify the two with the lawyer and follow them."

"It's these kind of fuck-ups that led to your losing two undercover agents," I seethed, furious.

"Quiet. Let me think."

I grabbed her by the shoulders. "Call off the operation but not our deal."

She looked at me for a fraction of a second. Long enough to tell me I had to run. Right away. Lucky for me, I'd already staked out a hideout.

I slipped out of the elevator and made for the door. All of a sudden someone came up behind me and planted the barrel of a pistol square in my back.

"Walk," said a voice in English.

I turned to see Marino had also been blindsided and was being led forward.

As soon as we were out on the street a white van pulled up. When the side door opened I found myself facing Paz Anaya Vega, a silencer pointed right at me. She looked like hatred itself.

I wanted her to kill me then and there, but it wasn't my lucky day.

Six

I t was raining, for a change. Julie Rhodes was singing "I'd Rather Go Blind," and I was looking out the window with a cigarette dangling from my lips and a glass of Calvados in my hand, waiting for Pierino Martinenghi to call.

His prostitute friend was willing to talk to me about Edith, but in return she needed to be sure she'd be safe. She promised to be in touch soon, but Vienna was a zoo those days, a carnival for tourists, and work had picked up substantially.

After the meeting with Paz Anaya Vega and her crew, we'd laid low to avoid any surprises from the Spaniard or Dottoressa Marino.

We were convinced that that lady cop would be after us the moment we were back in Italy, maybe treat us to a surprise search and seizure, during which those three kilos of cocaine she'd threatened us with would appear.

That was why we were in no rush to cross the border. Even Inspector Campagna agreed. Our hope was that the Spaniard would nab Pellegrini and send his operation into a tailspin.

Our plan wasn't great. But it was the only option. We'd gone over it again and again, scrambling for alternatives that didn't exist.

Then there was Edith. I didn't want to leave Vienna and face what was coming to us before explaining to her that I wasn't the person she thought I was, especially without having had the chance to offer her our help. I had no doubts that the gang of pimps she worked for had done her harm.

"He'll call, don't worry," said Beniamino, sitting on the couch with the Italian paper from the day before. He removed his reading glasses. "And take it easy with the Calvados. It's eleven in the morning."

I pretended to blow him off with a wave of my hand.

"You can drain the bottle, but if you don't have a clear head, I'm not leaving the house. Now's not the time to mess around."

I emptied my glass in one swig. "That was the last," I said. "Now I'm going to Max for reinforcements."

The Fat Man was in the kitchen writing a long email.

"A woman?" I asked, fumbling with the coffee machine.

"I met her in the mountains when I took off to work at a retreat," he said, still typing away. "I'm trying to tactfully figure out if she's still free. I'd like to spend summer in the Dolomites again."

"Lacanian shrink?" I asked, recalling his passion for the type.

"No, I gave that up," he joked. Then he thought again. "To be honest, I've never met another."

"Maybe they're extinct."

He wagged his big index finger.

"Impossible. I probably haven't tapped into the right circle yet."

"So you woke up this morning all optimistic and realized you still don't have summer plans," I said, needling him.

"I wouldn't go so far as 'optimistic.' More like in a good mood," he replied, pointing to the oven. "On the third try, the Wiener Brot came out perfect. Try it."

Max had become obsessed with the dish, a cross between a baguette and a brioche.

"I don't think I've digested yesterday's effort."

"There's butter and bearberry jam in the fridge," he continued, undeterred. "Besides, you still haven't had breakfast and the booze on your breath is stinking up my kitchen."

"Don't you start," I protested.

"Get a move on. I've got to prepare lunch in a minute."

"Another local recipe?"

"No, Venetian. And fit for a dreary day: bean soup, orzo, and crackling. Gialèt della Valbelluna would be the best variety, but we'll make do with some first-rate borlotti."

I felt I ought to change my mind. The bread was good, the jam not so good, but I forced myself to eat in order to stanch the alcohol. Max never stopped tapping away at the keys.

"Are you still writing that email?"

"Yes. It's been a while since I was last in touch and I've got a lot to tell her."

"About the marvelous time you're having right now?"

He gave me a withering look.

"Don't be a pest," he ordered.

I gestured with my hands to say I was sorry. "I can't stop thinking about Edith," I explained.

"That's no reason to bother a poor guy who's struggling to reconnect with an intelligent, witty, tender woman. A *very* tender woman. I'm not sure you understand the kind of thrills I'm referring to."

"I can try."

"Because I can't update her on the more intimate twists in my life of adventure, all I can do is reflect deeply on the memories that we share," he explained, getting worked up. "But I risk sounding tedious. What kind of woman wants to go to bed with a bore?"

"I don't understand why you're getting so worked up."

"Because you're distracting me and writing requires concentration."

I made a gesture of zipping my mouth. I'd seen an old Argentine woman do the same many years ago and it struck me as being the most effective way of swearing that your lips were sealed.

I did the one thing that could help me abide the wait: I shaved and listened to good blues. I'd tossed a few albums at random into my backpack and found an old stereo with a CD player in the apartment. I decided on the joyful, passionate voice of Grainne Duffy and selected "Let Me In," the song I liked best, before filling the sink with hot water.

The Punisher Pierino Martinenghi didn't get in touch until midafternoon. I was napping when the electronic version of "Rosamunde" alerted me to the fact that things were finally moving.

"My friend Klaudia should be free around seven," he said. "She has to accompany a client to Sexworld Spartacus and then she'll meet you in front of Hotel Kummer, in Mariahilfer Straße. She said you might have to wait because the john's slow to make up his mind."

"How do we recognize her?"

"I'll send you her photo. I just took it."

Smart man—Pierino was always thinking ahead.

"I hope German's not the only language she speaks."

"If she didn't speak English she couldn't work the hotels. She speaks a little Italian too."

"Did you teach her?"

The safecracker laughed heartily before hanging up.

A few seconds later, I was scrutinizing the face of an attractive thirty-year-old on the screen of my phone. She had straight blond hair and a warm smile. Her smile was meant for my friend Pierino, evidently, a far cry from the kind reserved for paying customers.

I could have gone to the meeting alone, but my friends had decided to get involved in this Edith business, and it seemed only fitting that they get a sense of the person they were going to help. But they also had another reason for coming: when it came to a woman I liked, my judgment was never objective.

I went to the living room. Max and Beniamino were chatting about boats and the Dalmatian Islands. We all could have used some sun.

"Her name's Klaudia," I said, and showed them the photo.

I don't recall exactly how, but I managed to spark a heated debate about what would drive a man to have a prostitute escort him to the biggest sex shop in Austria. It all began with a couple of dirty jokes and had turned into serious reflection.

It was still raining when we walked out of the building. We shielded ourselves with umbrellas and walked to a taxi stand a safe distance away.

The driver was Algerian and couldn't take the dreadful weather any longer. He liked Italy but was convinced that the quality of life was better in Austria. "And Algeria?" asked Max. The man shrugged his shoulders and withdrew into an oppressive silence. I breathed a sigh of relief once I was out of the car.

Mariahilfer Straße was one of Vienna's major shopping arteries. The Hotel Kummer was old but respectable, and it boasted panoramic views on the top floors.

That info and more came courtesy of a shady, elegantly dressed guy who waylaid us the minute we entered the hall.

Once again I discovered that the word "scram" was universal. The man retreated quickly and in good order, maybe because Rossini was the one who put him on notice.

Pierino's friend arrived twenty minutes late. She was definitely striking. Tall, statuesque, she wore a long white overcoat with fur cuffs, parted to reveal a pair of boots that ran midway up her thighs, a miniskirt, and a shirt left generously unbuttoned. She was clad in tasteful Italian brands. She wore light makeup and her jewelry was almost invisible. You wouldn't automatically guess her profession.

"You're a real beauty, Klaudia," said Old Rossini after we'd introduced ourselves; there was nothing slimy about his compliment.

She thanked him and proposed we go to dinner in a traditional beer hall nearby.

She was a regular there. She greeted the bartenders and waiters and strode over to a less rowdy area where a few tables were almost all unoccupied.

"I only agreed to talk to you because Pierino asked," she said, immediately setting the record straight. "He's a good man and I'm very fond of him."

"We're honored to call him a friend," I asserted.

"I know. He told me to trust you, but Edith is a touchy subject and I don't want trouble."

"We just need some information."

"And I need honesty. Before I answer your questions I want to know why you're interested in her. You're Italian, and from what our mutual friend tells me, you're just passing through Vienna."

She was worried there was something else going on. She'd been around long enough to know that crooks have countless wiles, and she didn't want to get mixed up with criminal elements.

Beniamino and the Fat Man looked at me.

"Your turn," said Max.

I told her what went down. The first meeting at the hotel bar, the one after at the café. The words, apparently nonsense, that Edith had uttered in a fright.

"I like her," I admitted, sure that Klaudia would understand. "And if somehow she's being forced to turn tricks, we want to help her change her situation."

"My friend Marco isn't your average john. He doesn't lose his head over just any girl," interrupted Rossini. "And we're upstanding, old-school outlaws."

She picked up her glass and proposed a toast: "To love and

liberty," she whispered. "But your words don't mean a thing as far as poor Edith's concerned. You should forget her and go back home."

Exactly what I hadn't wanted to hear.

"Why?" I asked.

"Frau Vieira isn't bad for a madam. She runs a major escort service that gives her license to operate on other levels, understand?"

"She's capable of satisfying all kinds of demands."

"She treats us good, as long as we respect the terms of the agreement. And that's exactly what Edith Amaral didn't do."

One September day, when it was still warm enough to walk around outdoors, this john turns up. In no time they're meeting regularly. The man is kind, caring. He showers her with gifts. Prior to that, Edith had only been with Frau Vieira's men, because the madam insisted that the Portuguese in her employ only sleep with one another. This sweet man, who did everything he could to prove to her that he was hopelessly in love, was a breath of fresh air in a life that had become harder and harder to bear.

Edith capitulated. For the first time, she let her emotions hold sway. He wanted to take her away from Vienna and Frau Vieira. He fed her a plausible line about a pretty little cottage in Bretagne, a small tourist shop selling handicraft goods. Another country, another life. Love.

But in order to run away, and all that other good stuff, they needed money. And he didn't have any. Moreover, the little savings Edith had couldn't be used because they were tied up in stocks and bonds by a broker connected to the organization.

They had one shot at realizing their dream: rob the madam.

The guy knew that all the cash that the girls earned and the pimps collected was kept in a safe in Frau Vieira's office. Three times a month an accountant would pick up the money, but during the Christmas season all the earnings from December weren't touched until after the Epiphany.

A hefty sum, as Edith knew. She'd been fucked by the crew's deputies for so long that she knew all the details. Even where they hid the key to deposit the money during the day. The madam kept the other key around her neck.

It was a practical system, though hardly secure. But no one would dare try to pull off a job like that. The Portuguese, especially Luis Azevedo and Rui Salgueiro, had earned Frau Vieira the respect she commanded, breaking bones and creating the myth that they could make anyone with the gall to challenge her disappear.

It was up to Edith to decide. He didn't pressure her. He didn't need to. Happiness was within her reach and she knew that, for a whore who wants to change her lot, some opportunities only present themselves once in a lifetime.

On the night of December 31, while the world was ringing in the New Year, Edith slipped out of the broom closet where she'd hid all afternoon. She had gone to the office with some excuse. After exchanging a few words with Frau Vieira and one of her exes, she pretended to leave and then crept into that closet full of mops and buckets.

The key was in its usual place and, as fireworks illuminated Vienna's skyline, she opened the safe and stuffed the bills into her purse. The john was waiting for her in a car with their suitcases.

They entered the highway, having carefully planned their route. They'd cross Germany into France. He stopped at a gas station to fill up the car and asked her to go buy him cigarettes. By the time she got back, carrying two packs of Marlboro Reds and the violet mints she liked so much, he wasn't there. He'd left her.

Klaudia couldn't say what they did to her when she came back to Vienna. Rumors spread. The most credible was that she'd been locked in a basement, and after a few days her lover was brought in to keep her company. A corpse. His body pummeled.

Word had it that before he died the man had confessed to colluding with one of the pimps in the crew. In fact, one of them had vanished all of a sudden and hadn't been seen since. Apparently the plan had been his handiwork. They'd picked Edith because they figured she was the "right one," sensitive enough to fall for the oldest trick in the book: love.

Frau Vieira proved sympathetic. Edith could go on living as long as she paid back the money she'd stolen. Plus interest. The madam told the other girls that Edith would be her old whore forever. Forced her to become an outrageous character, verging on the ridiculous. Frau Vieira's henchmen made sure the johns didn't get too intimate. She condemned her to solitude.

"Her life's hell," said Klaudia, finishing her story. "We're all convinced that she'll go mad or take her own life."

Now I understood Edith's reaction when I'd mentioned her jailer. I looked at my partners. They both nodded: we'd go forward with our plan.

"We want to talk to her," I said. "Can you tell us where she lives? Or maybe you know another way of contacting her without putting her in danger?"

The girl looked perplexed. "I guess I didn't make myself clear. Frau Vieira won't ever let her go, she'd lose her reputation," she repeated. "And this time, the girl would die and you'd disappear in some ditch."

No one batted an eye. Klaudia looked us over, one at a time. "I don't get it. You should be afraid. Maybe you don't believe what I'm saying?"

"We believe everything you told us," the Fat Man assured her, digging into an extra-large portion of paprika-glazed ribs. "The fact is, we think trying to help Edith is worth it."

She pointed at me. "Just because your friend here likes her?"

she asked, in shock. "He's only seen her a couple of times." Then she turned to me. "You haven't even slept with her. What happens if you don't like her? Your story doesn't add up."

Klaudia was losing her patience. It was understandable. It wasn't easy to explain the meaning of an outlaw heart. Or that it was impossible for me to accept the idea that I couldn't court a woman just because she was the old property of a ruthless Portuguese madam.

Old Rossini saw to it.

"All we want is what's good for her. If that means forgetting having ever met her, that's what we'll do. But if there's a concrete, sufficiently safe chance of tearing her away from Frau Vieira, we're going to take it. And we're not going to ditch her at a gas station. We'll do everything we can to guarantee she has a future."

He placed his hand on my arm. "As for my friend, you should know that this is how he's fallen in love his whole life. He meets a woman he likes and loses his head. But there's nothing wrong with that either."

Klaudia smiled. She was still far from understanding our reasons but figured she could trust us.

"You guys are insane."

Max grabbed the handle of his stein. "To love, liberty, and insanity."

* * *

Edith lived in Lorystraße, on the first floor of a small apartment building with a sky-blue façade, down the way from a small park. Klaudia gave us the scoop about her shift: she started work in the early afternoon and left her last john at night. She'd also offered to talk to Edith about our meeting and put her at ease, but we refused, because that might put her in danger.

We'd improvise. The one spot that allowed us to surveil the door to her building was a vegetarian restaurant, which served us an excellent mid-morning snack of potato beer scones. The problem was they served non-alcoholic drinks only.

After exactly one hour of waiting, I proposed to go ring the bell. Maybe she'd let me in.

"She won't," wagered the Fat Man.

"She's still asleep," said Beniamino, raising the stakes.

"But if she goes out and we approach her on the street, she might freak and start screaming," I objected. "The last thing we need is to be stopped by police."

Fifteen minutes later Edith solved our problem for us when she stepped out of the building. She had on the same overcoat that she wore the day we met at Jonas Reindl Coffee. Only this time she had her hair down. She was beautiful.

I stood up. "I'm going to talk to her," I said, moved.

"No," Rossini countered firmly. "I'll go."

"But I know her," I protested.

"And she knows you," replied Max. "It'd be better if we played the kind and charming stranger card."

I watched Beniamino jog up to her and strike up a conversation. At a certain point my friend pointed to the restaurant and added a few words before she backed off, practically ran away. Our effort had gone up in flames.

"Things'll go better next time," said the Fat Man to console me.

The Old Gangster returned to our table, looking, all in all, pretty satisfied. "I told her I'm your friend, that you're not a prick, and that if she wants to meet us she can find us at this restaurant."

"Doesn't look like it worked," I said, discouraged.

"She's a woman who's been through terrible experiences, who's living in terror now," replied Rossini. "She needs time to think and figure out that she can trust you."

"Beniamino's right," Max weighed in. "Giving her the chance to decide was a smart move."

I looked at the street. Edith wasn't coming back. "O.K. We'll wait and hope," I conceded, something polemical in my tone.

The waitress came over. Twenty-something, her red hair parted in two messy braids, on her left wrist a tattoo of a community center in Berlin. "We're about to start serving lunch," she announced, as if she harbored doubts about our sense of time. "Are you going to free the table or should I bring you a menu?"

"We'll eat here," I hastened to say, casting a cool look at Max. You never knew with him where food was concerned.

"I've got nothing against vegetarianism," he said testily while perusing the day's specialties. "In fact, I agree that the consumption of meat is excessive, and that a diet light on—not deprived of—animal protein can be beneficial—"

"Quit while you're ahead," said Beniamino with a smirk. "You're not fooling anybody."

To spite us the Fat Man ordered vegan. I let myself be enticed by the barley soup.

At some point I looked up from my dish and saw Edith staring at me through the window. With a conspicuous wave of his hand and a broad smile, Old Rossini invited her in. But she retreated again.

"She'll be back," bet Beniamino.

He was right. Five minutes later she was sitting at our table.

"What do you want?" she asked, her voice trembling. "If Frau Vieira didn't send you then how do you know where I live?"

"So many questions!" cried Rossini jovially. "Why don't you have a bite to eat while we explain everything?"

She shook her head. She was too nervous. We were frightening her.

"We know what happened to you," I said. "We're not mixed up with Frau Vieira or Luis Azevedo or Rui Salgueiro. If you want, we can help you build a life somewhere else, where no one will think they have the right to decide what you do with your body."

"Why do you want to do that for me? I'm just Frau Vieira's old whore."

"To us you're Edith Amaral," I shot back.

"So? What's that supposed to mean?" she demanded.

We could have bandied about big meaningful words, appealed to the ideals of humanity. She would have laughed in our faces. Hookers are the kind of people who feel cheated on principle. Edith most of all.

"My woman used to work strip clubs. Her name was Sylvie," Beniamino began. "She was a burlesque queen. Hated pimps. More than once, with my support, she helped girls get out from under their exploiters. Then I had to kill a man, and in retaliation she was kidnapped and surrendered to a crew that rented out women for certain kinds of parties. She was forced to dance, and afterward they'd gang bang her. We managed to free her, and I killed everyone who'd done her harm. But Sylvie couldn't forget the violence she'd suffered. My love wasn't enough, and in the end she killed herself."

The Old Gangster's eyes were full of tears. He reached his hand out to Edith. "I can't sleep at night knowing there are people out there like Frau Vieira. When they cross my path, I don't duck them. You're the old whore I want to rescue from her."

Edith sighed and shut her eyes. She knew the man in front of her was telling the truth, but she still wasn't ready to risk it. "There's no way of escaping the Frau. She'll kill us."

Rossini gripped her hand hard and forced her to look at him. "They're the ones that need to watch their backs."

She smiled bitterly before standing up.

"I don't know what to think," she confessed. "It's all so absurd."

"Where do you want to go?" I asked. "Do you want to go back to Portugal?"

"There's no one there for me anymore. I'm dead to my family."

"Where then?"

"I don't know. I've lived in Austria all my life."

"I could take you around the world. That way you could choose a place that you liked."

Another smile. More bitter than the one before. "I've got to go."

I followed her. "I'd like to see you again," I said as she headed home.

"Who? Edith or Tempest Storm?"

"As a pin-up you're a knockout, but I prefer this you."

"Then it won't happen. Frau Vieira won't allow me to see anybody outside work."

"I don't want to pay to sleep with you. I'd like the chance to see you again."

She pointed to a bar a few hundred feet away. "Tomorrow morning at ten. O.K.?"

"I'll be there," I cried, happy as a boy. She shook her head good-naturedly.

I could have kissed her on the cheek, but after hesitating a minute I turned and walked back.

My friends had left the place and were enjoying their first cigarette in several hours. The restaurant was one of the few to have banned smoking.

Rossini still had tears in his eyes. It takes a long time to recover from pain of that magnitude.

"Thanks," I said softly.

"For what?"

"For finding a way to speak on Edith's level. I know what it cost you."

He changed the subject. Just as I expected he would.

"It's useless to continue to torment her," he said. "She's too scared to make decisions that important. It's clear she wants to be rid of the scumbags draining her life, but she won't do anything to save herself."

I drew a cigarette out of the Fat Man's pack. "It's up to us. As long as we figure out a way not to get killed."

"We have two options," the Old Gangster chimed in. "The first is we steal her from under their nose. There's always that convent in Croatia where the nuns took care of the girls Sylvie and I used to bring them."

"And the second?" implored the Fat Man.

"We do things the right way," replied Beniamino with a malicious smile. "We go see Frau Vieira and plead our friend's case. The madam tells us to fuck off, we take offense, and we make it clear to her she's in the wrong."

"Gut reaction, I prefer the first scenario," I said. "In our situation, we're better off not drawing the local cops' attention. According to Martinenghi, they have a good relationship with the Portuguese madam and her crew."

"Speaking of, did you ever hear back from Campagna?" asked Max.

"I switched off the phone," I admitted. "I don't feel like listening to his bullshit while we're tied up with other business."

"Well, you should be in constant contact with him, Marco," lectured Rossini. "We need to keep an eye on what Dottoressa Marino is up to."

"I'll take care of it tomorrow morning, after I've had breakfast with Edith."

"You managed to score another date," complimented the Fat Man.

But Rossini advised me, with venom in his voice, "Try not to make her run away like last time."

He was pissed that I hadn't been monitoring the business

with Paz Anaya Vega that had brought us to Vienna in the first place. I should have apologized and called the inspector, and instead I was failing to appreciate our situation because I was caught up worrying about Edith's fate. And my love life. I knew that, but right then all I wanted was to listen to my heart as it pounded out a twelve-bar blues. It was a bad idea but, you know, sometimes common sense fucks off elsewhere.

With the other phone I called Pierino Martinenghi.

"We need to see you."

"Then you can buy me a drink. I get off before dinner."

We met the safecracker at a wine bar in Singerstaße. Pierino had had time to change; he wasn't sporting that ugly hotel uniform anymore.

"What are we drinking?" asked Max, scoping out the bottles on display.

"I'll start with a bottle of Silvio Nardi '43': Sangiovese, Merlot, and Petit Verdot. Then I'll take a Brunello di Montalcino, the Manachiara, from the same estate."

"You want to spoil us," I joked.

"To be honest I want to pamper myself while I wait to hear what kind of jam you're planning to put me in," admitted Pierino with a sly smirk. "Yesterday you had dinner with Klaudia and, lo and behold, today you're dying to talk to me. I mean, first it's drug dealers, then it's Frau Vieira—you don't want to miss out on any of the action in Vienna."

Beniamino held his hands out. As he should have.

"If you don't want to touch the subject we can drink to each other's health and go back to being friends like before."

Martinenghi frowned. "Thanks for the courtesy, but I want to hear what you have to say, then I'll decide what to do," he explained calmly. "For the record, I hate pimps too. Working in hotels, I've been forced to witness scenes that have left a mark right here," he added, touching his chest at the height of his heart.

"I'm glad we're of the same mind, though I didn't have any doubts to the contrary," continued Rossini. "We've decided to draw Edith from the deck."

"So where's the problem?" asked Pierino.

"If she disappears, the other girls will think it was the work of their protectors, done to punish her," I answered. "We want to avoid consolidating their power."

The safecracker stuck his nose in his glass and breathed in the wine's bouquet. "I get it. You want to save Edith and at the same time damage the crew's rep."

"Damage of a certain scale," I stressed. "All of Vienna needs to know. It's got to be the biggest story of the year."

"Frau Vieira will involve the cops. She's got several on her payroll."

"We don't plan on sticking around long."

Martinenghi picked up a slice of prosciutto and began coiling it around a breadstick with painfully slow precision. He needed time to think. He knew that helping us put him in a thorny position. If not a dangerous one.

"I'm planning a score," he confided, a spark of excitement in his eyes. "A beautiful safe from the 1970s, all gears and levers, none of that electronic crap. I've already cracked two of the same model, but this young widow was modified twenty years after. It's a challenge I can't give up—and won't."

"We get it. It's not a problem," said Beniamino.

"Yeah, it is a problem," replied Pierino. "It wouldn't be honorable of me to abandon you right now. We've always been loyal to an idea of criminality that despises scumbags."

I looked at my friends. "You've already done a lot for us," I said with a certain amount of embarrassment.

"Out of friendship," he added.

"What about the safe?"

He stretched his arms. "It can wait. And if I have to bag the whole thing, I'll look for another one."

"But if you stick to playing a minor role, they might not discover you were involved," remarked Max. "What we really need at the moment is information."

The waiter, a Tuscan in a Tuscan joint, interrupted to bring us the second bottle—a Brunello di Montalcino Cru—and fresh glasses. "Eighteen months in barrique, twelve in a barrel, and aged two years in the bottle," he said with a certain solemnity, fearing, perhaps, that we'd guzzle it down without savoring it.

I took a sip. It was a really intense, complex wine, with clear hints of ripe fruit. It should have been reserved for a more cheerful occasion, but we managed to appreciate it properly.

Pierino countered the Fat Man's argument with a sensible, practical consideration. "Portuguese mobsters are just like all the rest. When someone cons them and they don't know who, they get to thinking, they turn over every stone, they check every contact. And in the end they put two and two together."

It was true: that was exactly what they were like. Criminal organizations like that can't afford to let mistakes go unpunished.

At that point Beniamino wanted to rethink the whole situation. "Maybe we ought to go back to plan A: Edith disappears, and no one risks getting hurt."

Pierino was the first to object. "I had coffee with Klaudia after lunch. She told me what happened to Edith. I'd rather not be involved, but it hurts knowing those crooks can exploit girls with the help of cops and get off scot-free."

There was nothing left to add. End of discussion.

"What do you want to know?" he asked.

I had two questions at the ready. "Is Frau Vieira the real head of the operation?"

"Yes."

"Who's she closest to? I don't mean relatives, I mean members of the organization."

"You're asking if there's someone she can't run the show without?"

"Exactly."

"Rui Salgueiro," he answered without hesitating. "Klaudia explained everything: Frau Vieira keeps everything in order and is in charge of the escort service—the legal front. But he handles all the rest."

"Klaudia said Luis Azevedo is the other heavy in the crew."

"He's just Salgueiro's right-hand man. A mindless proxy."

Max ran a search on his tablet and pulled up a photo of Salgueiro from an old assault case.

"It's an old photo, but he hasn't changed much," confirmed Pierino.

"And where can we find dear Rui?" asked Rossini.

"After dinner he hangs around Maxim, a nightclub in the middle of town, on Kärntner Straße, but his 'office,' where he conducts all his business, is in the back of a dive he owns, tucked away on a side street. It's called Leiria, in honor of the city all the Portuguese in his crew come from."

"And Edith," I said.

We paused for a moment, moved on to simpler subjects, like wine and the beauty of the Tuscan hills. Martinenghi called the owner over to our table, a woman from San Quirico d'Orcia, who immediately had a sample of *pici al ragù di cinghiale* brought over. Our friend introduced us as clients of the hotel, and the woman didn't press him for more details. But she was determined to talk about the current political situation in Italy, and our pleasant chat grew stale.

"It's always the same story with our compatriots," Pierino remarked. "They left Italy because there wasn't work or they weren't making a living and they're always quick to bad-mouth the government, rightly so. But if an Italian expresses a negative opinion about his own country they get pissed and refuse to even greet you. I prefer to keep my mouth shut. After all, I'm never returning to that backwater. The first safe to get cleaned out, the cops will come to take me away."

Me? I couldn't wait to cross the border again, because Edith would be there by my side. I began to daydream, and the Brunello helped, but Martinenghi dragged me back to reality.

"I take it you've already got a plan."

Rossini gestured in response. "More or less. The goal is to knock them flat on their asses."

"Vienna's not used to a ruckus," remarked Pierino.

"We'll try to keep the noise down," promised the Old Gangster.

We avoided dropping a thousand euro at Maxim just to locate our man amid a throng of horny guys and half naked girls. Besides, there were too many security cameras and bouncers to devise a plan. We set our sights on Leiria. Two rooms, dim lighting. The few clients in the place were mostly men.

"I'm hungry," said Max, as if that were news. "The wine's doing dances in my stomach."

"I bet the food's no good here," said Beniamino. "But there's no harm in taking a look."

We were greeted by a woman in her sixties who pointed to a table. The tablecloth was in sore need of a wash and the woman wiped off the crumbs with a rag that she kept tucked under her arm.

She only spoke German, but the menu was in five languages. Nearby two large, heavyset men were packing it away. The Fat Man asked them what they'd ordered and we voted unanimously to trust them: roast pork with rice pilaf and potato salad. And three large light beers.

The chef's assistant saw to serving us, a kid no older than eighteen with a flower-print bandanna who exited the kitchen loaded up with plates.

Right away we noticed a conspicuous stream of men passing by the restroom and entering a door labeled PRIVATE.

"The office is open," I mumbled.

I got up to go to the bathroom, whose cleanliness exceeded my rosiest expectations. I lingered in front of the other door just long enough to hear several people talking, and went back to my friends. I'd been tempted to pull the old "Sorry, wrong door," but that wouldn't fly with hardened criminals; it's in their nature to be suspicious.

The food turned out to be better than average. Were it cleaner and had it adequate service, the restaurant might have a shot at being flagged by one of those specialty sites and attracting a couple more customers. But on second thought, management couldn't have been all that interested in food and wine, seeing as the lion's share of their profits came from exploiting prostitutes.

A little later a couple came in. They were seated in a corner set apart from our room. He must have been 35 or 40. She was much younger, under 25 maybe. Wheat-blond hair, tarnished by a few pink highlights. She took off her long down jacket to reveal a skimpy dress, cinched at the waist by a large leather belt. Unlike her coarse face, her body was very attractive.

"Hungarian," said Beniamino after hearing them talk.

They gave the impression that they were waiting for someone. They ordered drinks, and he kept checking his watch and looking up at the door. The girl was glued to her phone.

"The son of a bitch brought his mare to the market," said the Old Gangster bitterly.

There wasn't any doubt about it. We couldn't say for sure how the man had convinced her to come with him to that restaurant, but clearly he was selling her to Frau Vieira's organization. Maybe he'd already had her slagging for a while and had realized he wasn't tough enough to match the competition. The one thing pimps were good at, generally speaking, was manipulating the women that turned tricks for them, roughly meting out violence and flattery. But they were reluctant to risk getting stabbed to defend an inch of the block. They only became dangerous when they assembled a crew like Frau Vieira's. Maybe the son of a bitch was looking to get hired and had shown up with the blond woman as a gesture of goodwill.

The boy with the bandanna cleared our table and came back with three helpings of sweet dumplings stuffed with soft cheese topped with a blueberry sauce. We pointed out that we hadn't ordered them.

He shrugged. "We had extra. Crazy Dominick always fucks up when he mans the fryer," he explained before walking away. Dominick must have been the cook. Relationships in restaurant kitchens can be complicated.

The sweets were delicious, in any case. Unfortunately we didn't get to sample them properly, because in walked Rui Salgueiro. We recognized him immediately. He wasn't wearing a coat, clear proof he'd come from the "office." He went over to the counter where the woman poured him two fingers of Asbach, a cheap brandy popular in Germany and Austria.

He stopped to check out our table. He'd never seen us before, but the way we were all laughing, as if one of us had just told a joke, convinced him we were harmless.

He was over 50. Not tall but burly. Bit of a paunch, the rest muscle. His skin was olive colored, his face like a peasant's from a bygone era. He wasn't good-looking but he could pass for alluring. You could tell he was a pimp by the way he dressed. Flashy clothes are their trademark. He didn't rise to the level of a French *macrò*, but the snug red shirt, open at the chest to show off the typical gold cross, and the nut-brown

pants tucked into his polished boots—they didn't go unnoticed. In his left hand he held a pack of cigarettes and a solid
gold lighter. On the middle finger of his right hand he wore a
massive ring with the head of a tiger; it must have left a mark
on more than a few faces.

Just as we'd imagined, he walked over to the table where
the couple was seated. The pair shot up, and the man greeted
him with exaggerated deference. The girl just looked embarrassed. Salgueiro invited them to sit down and began talking to
the man in hushed tones. The girl kept her eyes down. Every
so often her friend placed his finger under his chin and lifted
her head so that the Portuguese, who had yet to show an interest in the goods, could get a look at her.

It was heartbreaking to watch. Beniamino was stone-faced.
He watched the scene with a troubling look in his eyes. He was
reliving the hell of Sylvie. She, too, had been sold. The deal had
probably been struck in a joint just like this one. I turned to him.

"Would you rather we left?" I asked in a calm voice.

He gripped my arm. It hurt but I didn't move a muscle.
"No, we stay," he replied. "Tonight the trafficker gets what's
coming to him."

"Seems just to me," I said.

"Just," he repeated. "Just, motherfucker, just!"

I exchanged a look with Max, who had been looking on. He
sighed. A moment later, I did too. Rui Salgueiro decided he'd
had enough. He stood up, shook the guy's hand, and motioned
to the girl to follow him. She turned to look at her friend, who
urged her to get moving. Either the Portuguese wanted to sample the goods or he wanted to put her to work immediately.

The other man stayed there nursing his beer alone. He had
a perplexed look on his face, maybe the exchange hadn't gone
down so hot.

After a while he stood up, put on his heavy sheepskin coat,
and headed for the door.

Beniamino did the same, giving the guy a few seconds head start.

"Settle up," I told the Fat Man. "And go home."

Night. Cold. The shoplights switched off. Ditto the blinding lamps and neon bar signs. It was the worst area to teach some piece of shit a lesson. I quickened my pace to catch up with my friend.

"I can handle this myself," he said drily.

"What's the harm in me tagging along?" I replied. "That way I can keep a lookout for cops. It could happen. We're still in the center of a European capital."

He flew into a rage. "Are you trying to tell me I'm doing something stupid?"

"No. But I would have preferred this to go down in the dark of winter on the outskirts of town."

"It'll look like a mugging."

Stellar idea. It meant that he was meditating on what to do and that his mind wasn't completely clouded by pain and rage.

A square. A large church. The man made the mistake of hugging the side of the building. The Old Gangster covered his face with his scarf and ran up behind him without the man's ever noticing. One shove and the man tumbled in the shadowy corner of the bell tower. He got up and tried to run. Rossini stood in his way and brandished his fists.

"Put 'em up," he said calmly.

The other man accepted the challenge. Biggest mistake of his life. Beniamino hit him repeatedly in the face and ribs. When the man fell to the ground, Beniamino wailed on his legs. Sixty seconds the man would never forget.

Then Beniamino knelt and searched his jacket and pants pockets for the man's wallet.

"That's that," he said, short of breath. "Three months in the hospital at the least."

A few minutes later we came across a dumpster next to the service entrance of a bakery and seized the opportunity to get rid of the loot.

"Toss the gloves and scarf too," I said, "they're covered in blood. And tomorrow you'd better buy another coat."

Back at the apartment, Max greeted us in silence, trying to guess from our looks if things had gone smoothly.

We sat down at the table and drained a couple of glasses to alleviate the tension and the chill in our bones. The Old Gangster held his head in his hands. His shoulders shook a little.

I took the bottle of Calvados and stood up. I was in pieces. All I wanted was to have another drink and sleep until I had to get up and see Edith.

But there was something I wanted to say to my friends. It had crossed my mind while I'd watched Rossini tear that scumbag apart.

"Things have gotten out of hand, and now it's too late," I mumbled. "All we can do is hope our end isn't too painful. Before that happens, I'd like to set a few things straight, saving Edith first and foremost."

When I woke up the next morning, the house appeared empty. The door to Beniamino's room was wide open. The Fat Man's was shut. He was probably still sleeping. The same old coffee, the same old first cigarette of the day, staring out the window. Comforting habits in a life that was anything but. I was used to anxiety. I knew its every nuance, but that morning it was almost unbearable. Not even the blues helped. And yet I let the voice of the Cowboy Junkies' Margo Timmins wash over me, singing "Postcard Blues" and "Walking After Midnight."

The anxiety that morning couldn't be attributed to what happened the night before or my upcoming meeting with

Edith. It came from my own shady depths, which I had never wanted to explore. So now I could do nothing but let it have its way with me.

I dressed nicer than usual and removed a bottle of cologne from the bottom of my bag. The kind saleswoman at the perfume shop in Padua, who sold me expensive shaving products, had assured me women liked it.

On my way out I encountered the Fat Man in the kitchen. He was in his pajamas making breakfast.

"You'll court her until she capitulates and falls into your arms, am I right?" he said in a pale imitation of a dramatic voice.

"That's the intention."

"Well then, good luck."

He'd slept on the wrong side of the bed too. I left without saying goodbye.

I had time and looked for a taxi stand even farther than the usual spot. The sky was still gray but the people I passed by weren't carrying umbrellas. If the Viennese were sure it wouldn't rain, you could be confident it wouldn't.

I entered the bar where I was to meet Edith. I was two minutes early. I told the elderly waiter that I was waiting on someone. But after a half hour she still hadn't shown up. It was clear she wasn't coming. I was at a loss. I hadn't considered the possibility of her changing her mind, since she was the one who had chosen the time and place.

I smoked a couple of cigarettes outside the door of her apartment building and worked up the courage to ring her bell.

"Is that you, Marco?" she asked over the intercom.

"Yes."

"I'm not feeling well. Let's meet some other time."

"Let me come up."

Silence. But after a while I heard the door click open.

She lived on the second floor. I was barely up the first flight of stairs when I found myself standing face to face with her. She had on a black slip, there were still traces of pin-up make-up on her face.

She let me in, shut the door, and went back to bed. I watched her walk the length of the hallway to her room. I waited a moment for her to say something to me, then took off my parka and followed.

A little light filtered through the shutter, and she lay on her side with the duvet tucked up to her neck. I removed my shoes and stretched out beside her, terrified she'd kick me out.

She didn't. "Sorry. I had a difficult john yesterday. He hurt me, and I'd prefer to stay in bed."

"You don't have to explain. I don't want to hear about it anyways."

"If you insist on courting a whore, you have to bear the burdens of the job."

"You're right. If you're up to telling me what happened, I'll listen."

She rubbed my face in every last detail. She wanted to test how much I really cared, to see if I'd still desire her after knowing that she'd been with a man who was infatuated with dilation. Every time she saw him he'd bring certain toys: the bigger they were, the more he paid. Because Edith couldn't run the risk of his complaining to Frau Vieira's minions, she couldn't refuse.

The body of an old whore is no longer protected by the prospect of its being exploited for a long time. It's at the mercy of money, and the price is set by the client's fantasies.

I was perfectly aware of that from the moment I saw her at the hotel bar. But I didn't know how to tell her.

"Do I have to pay to hug you?" I asked.

She chuckled and rested her head on my chest. I caressed her hair and, seeing as she didn't protest, her face too.

"Is Marco your real name?" she asked all of a sudden.

"Marco Buratti."

"And do you have a family waiting for you somewhere?"

"In this world, all I have are two friends and a bunch of exes."

"What do you do for a living?"

"You must really like me," I joked, "otherwise you wouldn't be asking all these questions."

"Please answer me. Paz Anaya Vega doesn't meet just anyone. You must be some kind of kingpin."

I'd been waiting for her to ask. I hadn't been able to erase the memory of her look of disgust when she saw me talking to the Spaniard.

"I don't deal drugs. They make me sick," I replied. "I'm a private investigator without a license. I handle cases off the books, and the money I earn rarely comes from legit sources."

"Were you in jail?"

"Seven long years."

She let out a sigh of disappointment. "If I ran off with you I'd still have to turn tricks. I'm forty-two and in ten years I'll be a lot lizard—hunting for johns in gas station stalls. Ten euros for a blowjob, fifteen from the front, twenty from the back," she said, hard-bitten. "If I stay here nothing changes. I'll live out my last days in hospice if I don't die first."

She pulled away and coiled into a ball at the edge of the mattress.

At that point I stood up and put my shoes back on. "I'll take you away, Edith," I said. "You can't live like this anymore. With the help of my friends, I'll manage to find you an alternative, by which I mean a place to live and a job. Then you can decide what to do."

"And if I don't want to be with you?"

"I'll suffer the same as any spurned man, but it's not a bargaining chip," I answered before leaving.

I was happy to have seen her and told her that her enslavement would be over. For good. I wasn't expecting anything else.

I wandered around the neighborhood. I stopped to drink a beer and all of a sudden I remembered my promise to Rossini to call Campagna. I switched on the phone that we used to communicate and discovered that over the last twenty-four hours the inspector had tried to call me dozens of times.

"What's the point of having a phone if you keep it turned off the whole time?" he laid into me.

"Take it easy. What happened?"

"Are you still in Vienna?"

"Yes."

"I'm on my way. I'll call as soon as I'm off the plane."

He didn't sound like himself. He was palpably upset.

"Tell me why, otherwise you won't find me when you get here."

"Don't be a prick, Buratti."

"Talk. The line's secure."

"The Spaniard abducted Marino and Pellegrini. It happened in Munich. They were lured into a trap and fell for it like two fools."

My advice had worked: the Russian hackers had circulated the intel on Pellegrini and someone sold him out. It wasn't bad news at all. Sure, we hadn't planned for Marino to get mixed up in it, but it meant salvation for us and for Campagna. We were no longer at risk of ending up in jail in the Republic.

"You ought to be happy," I said. "We can turn the page."

"I can't do that."

"I'm sorry to hear. As far as I'm concerned, I'm going to spring for champagne and caviar and celebrate with my friends tonight," I said.

"I'm begging you, Buratti, I have to see you tonight."

"Sounds like you still need us," I remarked suspiciously. "I don't want to find myself back in the sorry situation of being threatened to do the dirty work for the ministry's super-cops."

"Not at all. I swear. On my daughter's life."

If I agreed to meet him and get involved, we'd most likely risk delaying our efforts to free Edith from the clutches of Frau Vieira. But in my world, a man doesn't swear on something that big for a lie or scam.

"All right," I conceded, "call me when you get in to the city."

Seven

L uckily the exhaust pipe runs along the wall behind me, otherwise I'd have frozen to death already. The problem is the nighttime, when they stop throwing wood on the fire and those bastards keep warm under the covers while I'm down here, naked and chained to a fucking rocking chair that teeters the minute I move.

They're holding Marino somewhere else. From time to time Paz drags her in and forces her to suck my dick, and when I come she squeezes my balls till I faint. She gets off on little, the Spaniard. She's devoid of imagination. Were I in her shoes, I'd have dreamed up a freak show.

If I'm not dead yet that's thanks to the Dottoressa's stupid idea to infiltrate Balakian's organization with me. And my ability to improvise quickly. When they caught us, the first thing I did was inform them that she wasn't my woman but an official from the Italian Ministry of the Interior.

Paz was addled with joy. She thought she'd won the lottery now that she had the chance to take revenge on the cop who had ordered the murder of her husband.

She'd wanted to celebrate with a blowtorch that she'd had made in an abandoned body shop on the outskirts of Munich. But her euphoria didn't last long: her men started bitching. They weren't so willing to blow their chances of cutting a deal with the cops and escaping the years in prison destined for them. They understood that their organization was through, and they'd come to terms with that, but the possibility of riding off into the sunset was too attractive to piss away by killing a cop.

They're still arguing. Paz must be in the minority at the moment, that much is clear, since the pretty Dottoressa hasn't seen a dick besides mine. She even has her clothes on still.

All things considered, they haven't gone too hard on me either. I doubt they're thinking of bargaining for my freedom, since I mean nothing to them, but they don't want to make any false moves right now.

We had only stayed in Munich one night. The next morning they loaded us onto another van and we drove for a long time, four or five hours at least. I'm positive we're in Austria now, since at a certain point the asshole driving the van and talking exclusively in German said "Salzburg." And the city of fucking Mozart is the first you pass over the border on the road that runs from Munich to Vienna.

From what I'd managed to spy under the blindfold that I had on for the entire trip, we must be in the hills or mountains, in a remote house surrounded by snow. The thought of making a run for it on foot was pointless. In order to pull it off, I'd have to kill them all, Paz and her three guard dogs. At first there'd been five of them, but two left. Probably to confer with the rest of the gang.

Every once and a while Paz whispers in Spanish the nasty things she has in store for me. For her satisfaction, I play along, but she doesn't frighten me. She'd already done the best she could do in the cellar of my restaurant when she killed Martina and Gemma. But on several occasions I've been far craftier, far more creative. Gifted. And that makes the difference, that separates her from me.

I've accepted pain, and she won't get anything else out of me. Had she delivered me the cocaine with Tobias that morning, I'd have taught her that when you strip someone's life away, you have to take possession of everything they have *inside.* If she were in my goddamn chair, we'd already have covered her childhood and adolescence. Paz can't even imagine the real pleasure of looking your victim in the eye when he realizes he's facing the mystery of the afterlife after he's been robbed of everything else.

And that's not my fate. It may be small consolation, but in the situation I find myself in, I don't see anything else that's positive. So far. Dying still doesn't suit me.

I have to piss. I have to shout loud and long, otherwise these guys will take their sweet time.

"Hello?! I can't hold it any longer!"

Here they come. The usual duo. I call them the "monks" because they don't say a word. They're ex-soldiers. You can tell by the way they move: cautious, rigid, methodical. The older of the two, a fifty-year-old with close-cropped white hair, I once saw with Slezak. He has snake eyes; likes to kill.

To carry me to the toilet they use a really ingenious system: a snare pole. They slip the cable around my neck, keeping me at a safe distance with the steel rod, and I follow their lead like a good pup.

I take the opportunity to stretch my legs. On my way back I pass by Paz. She doesn't even dignify me with a look. She's too busy on her phone.

Another couple of days and I'll have bedsores. I can already feel the blisters on my cheeks. The smell of food wafts through the room. Someone's cooking. They'll bring me leftovers. The other "monk" is supposed to spoon-feed me, but just as he's about to, he gets up and walks out. He figures feeding me isn't a necessity.

A car pulls up. Real big from the sound of the engine. The way he raises his voice, must be someone heavy. Paz stands her ground. Someone shouts in pain. They're working over Marino. Something's happening. Footsteps. Coming toward me.

Abo Tscherne: I know him well. Before meeting Tobias

Slezak, I dealt with him. The first idiot that I tricked into thinking I might be a good buyer. And then there's Paz, gripping the Dottoressa by the hair. Poor girl, they split her lip. Another guy comes in with a tripod and a video camera. Have they decided to film a porno? A collector's edition snuff film? It's a good joke, but I'll keep it to myself. I doubt they're in the mood to appreciate it.

The Spaniard picks up an old chair and forces the cop to sit next to me. Abo points to me and barks an order. The errand boy goes out to retrieve a blanket and covers my naked body. No, they're not interested in shooting just any flick.

Chairs are brought in for Tscherne and Paz. The red light of the camera goes on.

"Say your name," Abo orders the Dottoressa in the Italian he picked up in jail.

"Angela Marino."

"What's your rank?"

"Deputy Chief."

"What's his name?"

"Giorgio Pellegrini."

"Is he a cop too?"

"No. He's a wanted criminal."

"And what are you two doing together in Munich?"

"That's none of your business."

"But you were the one who furnished him with the new identity of Attilio Sforza and ordered him to kill Tobias Slezak and two of our friends."

"No, Pellegrini acted alone that time."

The bitch intends to stab me in the back.

"That's not true!" I scream.

Paz blows her top. She wants to tear out the liar's tongue, but they hold her back.

I can't understand what he's saying, but it's clear Abo's reprimanding her: now's not the time to lose your cool.

"Was she the one who gave the order to kill Tobias?" Tscherne asks.

"Yeah, I swear."

"And why would an Italian cop want three dead Austrians on her hands?"

"Keep your fucking mouth shut," whispers Marino.

But now doesn't seem like the right moment to. I answer him. I tell him everything I know. The cop isn't happy about it. She tries to interrupt me. But in a situation like ours, it doesn't pay to be a hero. And if I convince Abo that deep down I'm not such a bad guy, maybe I'll be spared Paz's torture and go out with a bullet to the back of the head.

"I suppose that the Austrian and German police know about your activities," says Abo, grinning broadly.

Marino doesn't answer. Can't answer. She changes tack.

"If you think you stand to gain something by bartering the life of an Italian official, I'd advise you to stop this interrogation," she says, recovering that arrogant vein that always set her apart. "The more details that emerge, the narrower your chance of a deal becomes, until walking away with your life becomes a luxury none of you can afford."

I look at her, amazed. Threats! Abo shifts in his chair. He's not as stupid or clouded by a thirst for revenge as the Spaniard.

"I can give you the name of a go-between to contact," adds the Dottoressa, "but you have to keep this business confidential. It's in everyone's best interest."

"And who would that be?"

"Inspector Giulio Campagna at Padua Central Police."

That's rich. I was expecting her to come up with Doctor So-and-So from the ministry. But a local cop is a shock.

Abo and the Spaniard go out to argue in peace. The errand boy filming the interview stays behind to guard us, but he's checking the quality of the video. He's distracted. And as far as I remember doesn't speak Italian.

"Campagna's a bit player," I say to Marino under my breath.

"I couldn't involve the men who are looking for me right now. Besides, Campagna's the right man: he's in contact with Buratti and his partners, and they know how to reach this fucking crew."

"There's some murky stuff in that little head of yours. While you wait for the rescue team, you open an avenue for diplomacy."

"Keep dreaming, Giorgio," she adds. "No one wants you alive."

I'd already figured as much, so I amuse myself by needling her.

"You're not tickled by the idea of me telling people how good you are at giving head?"

"Bet your ass I'm not."

The guard orders us to shut up. A little time passes before the bosses return to the room.

"It's a deal. We'll contact the cop and give him a copy of the video," says Tscherne. "We can be confident everyone will be satisfied in the end, since the Italian police can't allow it to wind up in the papers."

Paz snatches Marino by the hair. "Do you understand? It's not your life that's important but the fear of a scandal. That's the only reason you'll save your skin, but you better watch your back for the rest of your life, because I'm never going to forgive you."

The Dottoressa doesn't accept terms that easily. She wants to know, she won't relinquish control of the situation entirely. A cop to the core. "How did you find us?"

The Spaniard laughs. "Money. I paid some Russian hackers to circulate Pellegrini's photo online with a notice: 'Attention, Killer, Piece of Shit Colluding with the Italian Police.' The news went viral and interested parties sold you out."

So, Balakian made a small fortune. Six million of the ministry's slush funds, plus whatever Paz coughed up.

The Spaniard leads Marino out of the room, and I see my opening to talk to Abo. "Put in a good word with her for me?"

"I'm the grandfather of two children," he says. "Whenever I go see them, they cry because you made them orphans. And my daughter Sabine does nothing but ask me, 'Have you found Guntmar's killer yet?'"

Now I remember him. He was the youngest of the trio. I shot him as soon as I stepped out of the bathroom.

Abo puts his hand on my shoulder.

"Sabine is a strong woman. Just like her mother. There wasn't a woman in the Hells Angels with balls like her. The only thing I'll ask of Paz is your heart. Sabine will be happy to have it for a keepsake."

EIGHT

I nspector Campagna looked like a shadow of the man I'd met in Padua not long before. His puffy eyes glazed over, his beard grown out, his jacket and pants rumpled.

I agreed to meet him in an old beer hall in Rennweg, not far from his hotel. I was alone. Max and Beniamino refused to come with me. They didn't understand why I felt obliged to listen to what the cop had to say. We'd finally gotten out of the game and now we had to rescue Edith, deal a blow to Frau Vieira's organization, and head home.

Yet here I was, sitting in front of Campagna, confused to be staring at his cellphone and holding a pair of headphones that he'd handed me.

"What am I supposed to do with these?" I asked.

"Watch. More importantly, listen," he answered. "A package from Vienna containing a video card arrived at the station. Addressed to yours truly."

I took a sip of beer and did what he asked. The only two actors in the video were Marino and Pellegrini. She was disheveled, her lip swollen, and he was naked, tied to a chair, with a blanket covering him from the waist down. I watched and listened, and my stomach turned. I regretted not having listened to my friends.

"She's clever, the Dottoressa. Never fails to disappoint," I snapped. "You've at least figured out why she put you in the middle of this, I hope?"

He nodded. "Because we're the couple of the century: I'm

the way to get to you and you're the way to contact Paz Anaya Vega's gang."

"Have you shown the video to anyone yet?"

"Of course. I'm a cop, Buratti."

"Not the most clever one either. If you'd pretended not to have received it, we'd all have made out just fine."

"I know a senior official in Rome," he began. "A good guy, someone I trust blindly. He used to live in Veneto, then he was promoted and transferred to the ministry. As soon as I discovered what was going on, I hopped on a train to go talk to him."

"And?"

"A shockwave has rattled the inner recesses of the ministry and more than a few heads are going to roll. Now everyone is saying that Marino is a hothead who acted alone and neglected to follow proper rules and procedures. Her whole team has been called back to Italy."

The wicked witch had been left to her fate, the operation never existed, some functionary would pay the price, and if a scandal were to erupt, the ministry had covered its ass and could now act indignant when the media started making speculations. Nothing new under the sun.

"What's the catch, Campagna?"

He tapped the screen of his phone with his index finger. He wouldn't stop. He couldn't find the right words. "We have to come up with a solution before this video gets to the media."

I scoffed. "And they sent you?"

So that's how things went. The heavy who had replaced Marino's boss, and who was now denying prior knowledge of his subordinate's plans, had read my file and discovered my role as mediator in jail. Campagna was tasked with "intervening" to ask me to initiate negotiations with Paz Anaya Vega.

"If things turn out badly, we're the scapegoats, right?" I asked.

"For what it's worth, I'll take all responsibility."

"But if I refuse they'll find a way to make me pay."

"Afraid so. You know how these things work."

I was furious.

"If I tell Rossini you've put us back in the tight spot that we'd just barely escaped, he'll take a notion to shoot you. And he'd be completely justified."

"By no means was it over, Buratti," Campagna shot back, raising his voice. Fortunately, the place was noisy and the patrons busy enjoying themselves. "Marmorato and Pitta saw Marino and Pellegrini being forced into a van. They recognized one of Vega's men. Sooner or later one of my colleagues would have come knocking on your door. You're lucky it's me in Vienna."

"Why's that?"

"Because I can guarantee that we'll stick to the terms of the agreement."

"How are you going to do that? Before today you were slated to share a cell with us."

"The senior official I went to see is old-school. He's not one of those fanatics who allow inept and dangerous functionaries like Marino to strike out on their own."

I pounded the table. "Cut the bullshit, Campagna. The truth is the operation nose-dived and the collateral damage could be incalculable. Otherwise there'd be no objections and Marino's career would've been made."

"Think what you want, the game is clean this time."

I needed to clear my head and step out of the place to smoke a cigarette in peace. The nightmare continued. And in some ways, the situation could turn out to be a trap with no off-ramp. It was necessary to clear up some aspects of our agreement before going any further.

I called Max. "I don't know how to say this," I began.

"The cop's put us in a bind."

"Nice and tight," I confirmed. "You've got to get over here. Right away."

"Is that really necessary?"

I didn't answer, just gave him the address of the beer hall.

When I returned to the table, Campagna was looking around, disoriented. "I've never been to Vienna," he confided. "This is the first and, I hope, last mission abroad. I'm not cut out for this stuff. I'm just a small-town cop."

I raised my hand to interrupt. "Are you looking for my sympathy?" I asked, bowled over.

He realized he'd gone too far. "I'm tired is all."

"My partners are on their way," I said. "And before they sit down at this table, you and I have to clear up the details of our arrangement."

"I thought they were already clear."

"You're the only cop of any nationality that we'll deal with."

He pretended to look around. "You see any others here?"

"You don't get it: only you and us from here on out," I reiterated. "We'll resolve the situation our way. Your colleagues have to keep away. No interference whatsoever."

He made an eloquent gesture with his hand. "A criminal affair."

"I already told you we're not criminals," I balked. "Enough with the insults."

"Sorry," he hastened to say. "But I want you to reflect on one thing. If we discover where they're holding Marino prisoner and need the help of Austrian police—"

"We're not the Seventh Cavalry Scouts. Nor are we the 'good' Indians hunting the bad to offer up their head on a silver platter."

"What the fuck does that mean?"

"We have nothing to do with you all. If you want to save Marino's ass, and we find a way to take care of this video business, because that's what the top brass is really worried about, you have to guarantee us total autonomy."

"They'll refuse."

"I doubt it. We're the only ones with a direct line to the Spanish crew. We know their internal problems. We can get results in short order. But we do things our way."

The inspector looked at the phone lying on the table between the beer and an empty plate. "I have to call the senior official," he said reluctantly.

"In a minute. I'm not finished."

"What else is there?"

"I want a copy of the video. Now."

Campagna blanched. "Are you kidding? I shouldn't have even shown it to you."

"Consider it insurance for the future," I explained. "Not because I don't trust your word or the word of your big-shot friend, but in your field, roles, command posts, and staff change too easily. And I have to be honest: if things get rough, we're cutting ties, and having that video is our guarantee that you won't even think about coming after us."

The inspector hesitated, but eventually made up his mind and forwarded the video to our secure phone. "The fact is, you're right," he admitted. "I can't speak for everyone, and if another Marino shows up, you better have a card up your sleeve."

"I'm guessing that you've already given a copy to a lawyer," I said, though I knew the idea hadn't crossed his mind.

In fact, he shook his head. "I should, shouldn't I?"

"Soon as you get home."

Campagna went outside to phone his boss. In the meantime my friends arrived. I raised my arm to get their attention.

"This city has become unlivable," Rossini remarked sarcastically. He was in a horrible mood. "You can't have a beer without bumping into a cop who wants to make your life hell."

"He's out on the curb arguing on the phone," added Max,

"jumping up and down like a madman. Care to tell us what the hell is going on?"

I filled them in, starting with the images from the interview with Marino and Pellegrini, and proceeding to summarize my meeting with the inspector. They mulled it over in silence while I ordered beers to slake their anger.

"We have the video," reasoned the Fat Man. "If Campagna comes back and tells us his bosses refuse our conditions, we stand up and fly south to Croatia for the winter. Everyone agree?"

Yes. We did. Campagna would draw the ire of his superiors, but that wasn't our problem.

"And if they accept," continued Max, "we have to choose which horse to bet on: Paz Anaya Vega or Abo Tscherne."

I'd met both of them and didn't hesitate to pick the ex-Hell's Angel. There was no way we could count on Paz; she'd pretend to accept a deal and then stab us in the back. And she could afford to, since she had the means of disappearing an ocean away. Tscherne, on the other hand, he was Viennese. His family lived in the city and he wasn't the type to go into hiding. And then there was his crew to consider. He'd threaten his hostage's life and raise the specter of a scandal to save his men. And become boss.

Campagna nodded to my friends and sat down. "A week," he announced. "That's the best I could do."

In reality it was more than enough time. This business had to be resolved immediately, in forty-eight hours tops. Any longer and it would be too late. But it wasn't bad news: if we failed, we'd have a good head start getting away.

"There's a ghost hovering over this negotiation that none of us will name: Pellegrini," remarked Max with a devilish smile. "May we know the official position of your bosses, Campagna?"

The inspector turned red and put his head down. Everyone

assumed Handsome Giorgio would never get up alive from the rocking chair he was chained to.

Old Rossini lifted his glass. "Fuck you, Campagna. When are you going to piss off for good?" he asked, sounding, all in all, good-natured. He felt sorry for the cop.

The other played along. "Soon as I get the chance, Rossini."

"Pay the bill and go get some sleep," I told Campagna. "We'll set up a meet with the bad guys."

While the cop walked slowly in the direction of his hotel, I had to wake Pierino Martinenghi from his hard-earned slumber.

"What's up?" he asked, alarmed.

"Do you know how I can get a message to Abo Tscherne before tomorrow morning?"

He paused a moment before rattling off the name of a hotel, a night porter, and an address. "Tell him you're looking for Roman and sit tight. You'll see, he'll turn up before too long."

Roman, an old acquaintance. He was one of the two goons that had kept Old Rossini company in the hall while I spoke with Paz. Underneath his short green coat, he was wearing all black, except for a ridiculous, fire-red leather cravat.

He stiffened at the sight of us. I stood up from the couch and walked over while my friends stayed seated and stared daggers at him. Criminals like him love that kind of crap.

The dealer seemed a little drowsy to me, and insulting him was maybe the right way to wake him up. "Are you just a nickel-bag peddler or do you actually count for something? Because I have an urgent message for Abo, but you don't look like a guy who has the boss's ear."

He puffed out his chest. "I can call him right now if I want."

"Tell him the man he sent the video to has arrived in Vienna."

By his puzzled look, I knew he couldn't make heads or tails

of what I'd just said. "Are you fucking with me? What the hell are you on about?"

"That doesn't concern you. All you need to know is that if Abo finds out you're standing around killing time instead of passing on the message, he'll break your arms."

"Wait here," he mumbled, unconvinced.

He called someone else—not Tscherne—and smoked in the cold while he waited. He received a few more calls after which he signaled for me to be patient. Finally the right call came through. Roman handed me the phone.

"Who is this?" asked Abo in German.

"The last time we saw each other we spoke in Italian," I said, letting him know who it was.

"So, you do work for the cops."

I hung up. I didn't hand the phone back to its rightful owner because I was sure Abo would call back. And if he didn't, fine, but you can't be a credible mediator if you let the interested parties insult you.

The phone rang after a few seconds. "You're easily offended," said the dealer.

"I've been asked to aid the friend of your guest to find a solution that would satisfy everybody," I said, keeping things professional. "I propose we meet tomorrow morning at eleven at the train station concourse."

"Which one?"

"Mitte."

"Say I was tempted to come, are you really in a position to guarantee our deal will be respected?"

"More than that, I'm your only hope, Abo."

"That a fact?"

He sounded dismissive; I had to convince him that I meant business. "There's a reason I contacted you and not the Spaniard," I said. "You don't really think that what you're holding is worth saving both your asses."

I heard the flick of a lighter and then the sound of him taking a long drag of smoke, filling his lungs. Now I had his ear. "If it doesn't work out with you, I can always contact her," I continued. "I bet she'll find this conversation interesting. At least it'll help reinforce her position inside the organization."

"It's a free country, everyone can do as he pleases," he shot back. "But if I were you I would bear in mind that Paz and I both have a copy of you know what."

I'd led him to the edge of the cliff. Now I just needed to get him to look down and see how high the drop was. "Speaking of, only one of you can hold on to it for insurance. The other won't be able to avail herself of it."

Silence. For a moment he stopped breathing. "Are you sure that's how *they* want to do this?"

"Think about it, Abo, they killed Tobias Slezak and your son-in-law for a lot less," I replied. "My job is to make sure everyone keeps their wits about them and no one winds up with his back to the wall and is forced to act foolishly."

"I need proof they're acting in good faith."

"They're ready to come to the table, but that all depends on you."

"What do you mean?"

"Now's the time to betray her, Abo."

I slept little and dreamed a lot. That didn't happen often. I was visited by people from my past. Prior to prison. I woke up feeling empty: the sting of conscience had that effect on me. I would have rather had a spiked coffee and gone back to bed, but I lay there attempting to re-litigate my case, repeating how young and reckless I was. And that there hadn't been enough time to set things right, because life waits for no one, and one way or another people shuffle off. And I had dragged my feet, and the things I should have said had gotten caught in my throat.

Instead I had to get up and prepare for the meeting that I myself had scheduled. I'd picked out a busy station, one monitored by dozens of cameras, military units armed to the teeth, and law enforcement agents belonging to every department from antiterrorism to narcotics. My intention was to leave a trail of the meeting. I could be sure it would be caught on tape, but some cop or crook might remember it too.

I also intended to dissuade Abo and whomever else from making any risky moves or pulling any funny stuff. We all had to compromise.

Because we couldn't linger out in the open like that, our meeting would be brief, no beating around the bush. Most illegal activities revolved around a staggering heap of idle chatter. Criminals did nothing but talk. Just like politicians. Maybe that was why the two were often considered interchangeable. Experience had taught me that the more you go on negotiating, the more likely you were to fail.

By then I had my head straight. If Campagna had my back, it might all go down smoothly.

I swung by in a taxi to pick him up. He climbed in before the car pulled up to the curb. His breath smelled of coffee and cigarettes.

He looked subdued but kept quiet, which wasn't like him. I made sure the cab driver didn't understand Italian before instructing Campagna. He listened distractedly. He'd convinced himself that he was a good cop lowering himself to cut a deal with the scum of the earth. A stain on his immaculate conscience. I decided to disabuse him of any illusions.

"Abo Tscherne helped mail the package to Padua," I said. "He raped, tortured, and murdered Marina and Gemma, Pellegrini's wife and lover. Remember that when you grant him immunity."

He spun around to look at me. "What can I do about it?"

"You could start by not acting as if you fell into this

business by accident," I shot back, "the poor inspector obeying orders because he's the low man on the totem pole who takes no responsibility for his actions. Well, today you're going to have to assume all the responsibility, today you're going have to wade knee-deep in blood and shit."

"You think I don't know that?"

I wanted to tell him he didn't have the slightest idea how much he was about to change inside. Nothing would be the same again. But Campagna was depressed, unhappy about the way he'd been forced to do his job, and I preferred not to rub salt in his wounds. In any case, before the day was over, destiny would hand him the bill to be paid in many small and convenient installments. I looked out the window. The sky was clear, and the people looked happy.

The drug dealer was punctual. Dressed in leather, his moustache waxed, his hands in his pockets. He swaggered toward us as if to remind us that he was holding a major bargaining chip. We stood in the middle of the concourse, a continual stream of people flowed by.

He pointed at the inspector with his chin. "You must be the heavy the Italians sent."

"That's me," replied the cop.

"Now that everybody's been introduced, let's cut to the chase," I said, taking charge of the situation. "In exchange for the hostage's life—"

"Two hostages," interrupted Abo.

"We're only interested in the woman," I said before continuing. "Bring her back safe and sound and the Italian authorities won't extradite you for murdering the women in Padua with the Spaniard."

"You've got nothing on me," he objected.

"I wouldn't be so sure," I replied.

He grunted his disappointment. "Go on, you haven't said anything interesting yet."

"All the charges, including drug trafficking, will be brought against Paz Anaya Vega and other members of the organization. You choose which."

"Me and my crew will be kept out of the investigation?"

"Exactly. You'll save yourselves, but don't even think of reassembling your gang the day after. You have to keep a low profile. It's part of the deal," I said, and to make sure I was clear: "It's non-negotiable."

"What else is non-negotiable?"

"It's up to you to take care of Paz Anaya Vega and the others. Everyone better believe they ran for good this time."

Tscherne nodded. He'd already reckoned on digging a few graves.

"I'll hang on to the video as insurance," he added, eyeing Campagna.

"We'll keep our word," stammered the inspector, white as a sheet. He hadn't planned on being mixed up in so much killing.

"It gets done immediately," I said. "The cop should be back in Italy tomorrow morning at the latest."

"Not possible," objected the drug dealer. "This needs to be done the right way."

"Bullshit," I snapped. "The truth is you're not in control of the situation."

I took Campagna by the arm. "Let's go."

Abo gently placed his big mitt on my chest. "Wait, let me think about it."

"There's no time for that."

"Paz is with the hostages," he explained. "She won't leave them for a minute. There are three men with her. Only one is on my side."

"And you and a couple of your men can't pay her a visit?"

"The Spaniard's as cunning as the devil, she'd figure something was up. She thinks I'm in the city attending to business while I wait to hear from the Italian cops."

"Well then, your errand boy is going to have to take care of it. Can he handle that?"

"Yeah, he's one of the best, but I need to find a way to tell him over the phone."

I raised my arms. "Maybe now's your chance, don't you think?"

Tscherne walked off to make the call.

"What the fuck are you doing?" faltered Campagna, sliding into a panic. "No one authorized you to negotiate those terms. Get the address off him and we'll send in the Austrian SWAT team."

"You're not on about getting the local police involved again, are you? The Spaniard must die and the plan followed to the letter," I explained flatly. "Otherwise it all goes awry and we end up in deep shit."

"You talk about killing people like it were no big deal."

"There's no solution that allows for respecting the most basic principles of your 'legality,'" I reiterated. "But that was clear from the moment someone permitted Angela Marino to launch her operation."

I pulled out a cigarette, stuck it between his lips, and helped him light it. "Besides," I added, "there were three people in the cellar at La Nena: Paz Anaya Vega, Abo, and someone else we haven't identified. The Spaniard will be the only one to pay for the murder of Martina and Gemma, but at least the poor girls will get some justice. And the death of Pellegrini will also be welcome."

The cop turned his back on me and took a few drags. Who knows what he was looking at or thinking? It would have been even more complicated had I explained to him that I'd given Tscherne enough rope to hang himself with. Tscherne felt safe, Pellegrini's death meant there were no witnesses left to nail him, and rather than disband the organization he'd consolidate it to conquer new shares of the market. That was the error that would spell his ruin: he didn't have what it took to keep afloat in the choppy waters of international drug trafficking. Campagna was light years away from that kind of criminal thinking.

Tscherne returned moments later. "My man says he'll do it during dinner," he said. "We'll post up a few hundred feet away. If all goes smoothly, we'll receive a call and go collect the hostage. Otherwise we'll have to finish the job ourselves."

"'We' who?" asked Campagna.

The drug dealer sighed. "I can't mobilize other members of the organization, obviously."

"This plan only works if it's kept under wraps," I stepped in, addressing Campagna. "Should something come up, there'll be three of you to intervene: you, Abo, and Rossini. Max and I will be there, but we're no use in a gunfight."

"Conscientious objectors?" mocked Tscherne.

"Something like that," I replied.

It was at that moment Giulio Campagna tried to torch the whole plan. "You're out of your minds," he began in pure Paduan dialect. "I'm not shooting anybody—in a foreign country no less—without a sliver of authorization or legal cover."

Luckily Abo couldn't understand a word. I talked the inspector down in dialect: "Quit making a scene. No one's asking you to be a gunslinger," I lied. "But if you keep this bullshit up, there's no way you're going home with Marino alive."

Abo eyed me suspiciously. "What the fuck are you on about?"

"Nothing important," I said curtly and switched the subject. "Now we have to decide where and when to meet."

A few minutes before 5 P.M. we arrived in the center of the village of Großebersdorf, followed by the car that Campagna had rented, which would convey Dottoressa Marino to the closest border, where she would be picked up by functionaries from the ministry. We were in the Superb. Me at the wheel, Beniamino riding next to me with his handguns in his coat pockets and extra magazines in his jacket, and Max navigating from the backseat, checking the route on his tablet.

I hankered to drink and smoke. And be with Edith.

"Killing your own partners while sitting at the same table, eating the same bread, is an atrocity only drug dealers could commit," said Old Rossini, disgusted, while I parked next to a fire station as per Tscherne's instructions.

"If Abo's man changes his mind, it's up to you to settle the account," I responded.

"I almost wouldn't mind. At that point we could tweak the finale."

"Take out Abo?" asked the Fat Man.

"Why not? The problem is I'm alone and outgunned."

"You can't count on the cop," I said.

Rossini moved his wrist, causing his bracelets to jingle.

"Here he comes."

Campagna opened the door and climbed in next to Max.

"I miss something?" he asked.

Beniamino turned and handed him a gun and a magazine.

"Do these duds still fire?"

"We'll find out soon enough," Rossini replied grimly to shut him up. It didn't work.

"This is all wrong," mumbled Campagna. "There's not a single thing right about this business."

None of us said anything back. Words no longer mattered. The time had come to act and pray that we'd get lucky. We smoked in silence, in the dark and cold. We didn't even have a clear idea where we were.

A little later Abo showed up in an off-road vehicle. Beniamino got out of the car to check that he was alone. With scum like that you can never be sure. Knowing my friend, I could tell he was looking for any "legitimate" opening to kill the drug dealer. He couldn't stand the thought that Tscherne might walk away from the murders of Martina and Gemma. Especially after the sexual assault they'd had to endure.

Tscherne started driving, and we followed. Our tiny, three-car convoy began to pass through towns, gradually ascending the hillsides buried under snow. Occasionally the headlights illuminated a sign for a winery. The entire area looked abandoned, but the countryside was merely following the rhythm of the seasons, and its inhabitants remained snug inside their homes in anticipation of the new day.

Abo turned onto a dirt road and stopped after a few hundred feet. He motioned for us to get out. This was the place where we were supposed to wait for the killer's call.

"The house is about three hundred yards away," he explained, "but we can't get any closer right now."

I checked the time on my cellphone: 6:12. They'd be sitting down for dinner soon. It was so cold out that I hoped Tscherne's man wouldn't wait till dessert to leap into action.

I realized that it would take time—how much I couldn't say—to recover from the downturn that my life had taken. And my friends' lives. Waiting in the dark for a drug dealer to kill his accomplices wasn't how I'd wanted things to go down. Despite all the reasons I could marshal to justify our being on that hill, I felt deeply dismayed at how cynical this business had made me.

In a matter of minutes human beings would be dead, thanks to a strategy that I had devised, patiently, and for irreproachable reasons. But it was the hard-heartedness with which I was confronting this epilogue that gave me pause.

And now that the floodgates of truth had opened, it wasn't hard to see that my infatuation with Edith was nothing more than the antidote to keep the poison, which was turning me into a different and lesser man, from reaching my heart. That outlaw heart, which enabled me to meet life with my head held high.

27 minutes later Abo's phone rang. "It's done," he said, and walked over to his off-road vehicle.

Our headlights illuminated the façade of an old farmhouse. A man stood in the doorway gripping a gun.

"Careful now," Rossini advised Campagna, dropping a round in the chamber.

Tscherne signaled to follow him inside. At the doorstep I traded glances with the guy who had done the dirty work: his eyes were cold and glassy as a reptile's.

The kitchen was infused with the smell of food and the stink of gunpowder. On the floor the bodies of two men shot in the head. Only Paz Anaya Vega was still sitting, wedged between a chair and the table. She'd taken two bullets square in the chest. In her right hand she still held the spoon she had been eating her soup with.

"Where's Marino?" asked the inspector.

"In this room," answered the drug dealer. His man fished a key from his pocket and quickly opened an old, solid wood door.

The woman had heard the shots and hadn't known what to expect. When she recognized Campagna, she let out a sigh of relief and collapsed on the bed. He ran over to make sure she was all right.

"We saved your ass, Dottoressa," I said loudly. "You're in our debt now."

She stared at me a moment, then lowered her eyes while Max took the opportunity to snap a few photos with his phone.

"Did you shoot Pellegrini too?" I asked the killer in English.

"No," the man answered, pointing to another room.

Old Rossini, gun in hand, motioned for him to hurry up

and open it. When Handsome Giorgio saw us, he was more surprised than Marino but quicker to take stock of the situation.

"It was you who screwed me over, right? I can't believe three idiots managed to fuck everything up," he began blathering, shifting like a condemned man in his rocking chair, which wouldn't stop moving up and down.

"Shoot this piece of shit," I told Beniamino.

"I don't shoot men who are tied up."

It was the second time that Rossini had the chance to eliminate Giorgio Pellegrini and, for one reason or another, refused to pull the trigger.

"You're joking, right?"

He took the gun by the barrel and held it out to me.

"You do it. Or ask Abo and his little pal to do you the favor. There are some things I won't do, and I'm amazed that you're surprised."

Our interlude amused Pellegrini.

"You guys are a couple of standup comedians."

"Well then?" goaded Rossini.

"You know I don't use guns," I said, forced to reiterate my position.

"Exactly. So don't try to decide for others."

Caught up arguing, we didn't realize that Marino had come up behind us. She darted forward, snatched the gun, aimed, and fired. Three shots in quick succession, but only one hit Giorgio Pellegrini, just above his stomach; the other two were lodged in the wall over his shoulder. The cop let the weapon fall to the floor and ran over to him.

"Fuck you!" she screamed in his face. "Fuck you!"

Campagna grabbed her by the shoulders and began shaking her like a dummy. "What the hell did you do?" he screamed. "What the hell did you do?"

Marino burst into tears. She was very different from the

woman we'd known before. This business had changed her too—had managed to break her.

"Make sure she resigns," urged Rossini, still incredulous, picking up the shells off the floor as a precaution.

"You'll see, the higher ups will jump at the opportunity to be rid of this basket case," replied the inspector.

I blocked him from moving. "See how easy it is?" I prodded. "Welcome to the real world."

"I'm done with this crap."

I laughed in his face. "Starting today your bosses will use you whenever they need someone who knows a shortcut or two. Once you set foot in this racket, you never get out."

The inspector shook his head before brusquely leading Marino out of the house. A moment later we heard the sound of the car driving away.

Pellegrini wheezed to the rhythm of the rocking chair. He must have been in a lot of pain. I turned to Abo. "You'll take care of this?"

Tscherne nodded. "Don't worry about it. I'll handle everything."

At dawn we were still awake, drinking and smoking in the living room of the hideout on Oswaldgasse, trying to flush out the right words, which had until then remained hidden in the dark.

"For the first time in my life I was forced to team up with cops and drug dealers," began Old Rossini, hoarse from fatigue and tension. "I'm well aware that we had no other choice and that we'd already resigned ourselves to 'go for broke,' but I want to be clear—"

"It won't happen again," Max preempted him, "that goes for me too. Over the last few years we've been sucked into a vortex of cases where the line between our principles and everything we can't abide has become thin, sometimes nonexistent."

It was my turn to say something. "The truth is that the world around us has changed. For the worse. And it's harder and harder to survive without stooping to make comprises."

"I agree," answered the Fat Man. "But maybe the time has come to admit our weakness and fragility. We need to catch our breath and think calmly about our future."

"We need money," Beniamino broke in. He didn't care for conversations that took a low-key or excessively intimate turn. "After we've brought Edith to safety, I'm going to find Luc and Christine. Appears they intend to clean out a jewelry shop around Tolone."

Luc and Christine were a couple of professional thieves, close friends of the Old Gangster. They adored him.

"I'm going to the mountains," announced Max. "A dear friend of mine wrote to say she wants to see me again."

For my part, I didn't have any plans. I had Edith. If she wanted, I'd follow her anywhere. Otherwise I'd return to Padua. The lawyers I knew there sent trivial cases my way, enough to make a living. Paid in cash fresh from the ATM in a parking lot or café.

I stood up and grabbed the bottle of Calvados. "This round of goodbyes is making me sad," I said before retreating to my room.

Sena Ehrhardt sang "Cry to Me." After that I sought refuge in the arms of Mary Gauthier. She knew what was what. "Walk Through the Fire" was just the blues to give meaning to the sadness weighing me down.

NINE

Vienna was strange, shrouded in fog. Not as thick as the fog clouding my head. I rang Edith's buzzer at ten sharp. Five minutes later I began to suspect she wouldn't let me in. As I lit a cigarette I saw a man climb out of a parked car and walk toward me. He didn't look threatening; in fact, he appeared glad to see me. He must have been a little over 65: thinning dyed-black hair, a puckered face, patent leather shoes, and gold rings on his fingers. A pimp.

"Paisà" he greeted me. It was the one word of Italian he knew; after that, he muddled his way through a mix of English and Spanish. "Thank God you arrived. I would have frozen to death waiting in the car."

"Who are you?"

"My name is Nuno. And you must be Marco, Edith's Italian friend, correct?"

I smelled trouble underneath the guy's cheerful facade.

"What do you want, Nuno?"

"Frau Vieira is very fond of Edith," he said, "and would like to know why you're so interested in her."

I pointed to the building. "Where is she?"

He smiled ambiguously. "Staying at the Frau's."

Things weren't supposed to go down this way.

"What the fuck happened?"

"You know how whores get," he replied, doing the wise old man bit. "They talk. Dear Edith thought she could spill her story to an old friend who works as a coat-check at a bar;

instead her friend turned around and reported it to Frau Vieira."

"What are you talking about?"

"About an Italian who wanted to help her change her life, take her abroad, you know, the usual rubbish that comes out of a whore's mouth."

"You'd know."

"Oh, I know," he replied. "Same as I know about men who string them along. They act like Prince Charming then ruin them, because they're egomaniacs and don't get what whores really need."

Listen to this piece of shit. I felt like knocking him in the face, but now wasn't the time. "I'd love to delve deeper into this philosophical side of sexual exploitation," I bit back, "but I don't think you tracked me down just to chat."

He changed tack. "Frau Vieira would appreciate a face-to-face."

"When and where?"

He reached into his pocket for his phone and walked away to talk in private. Useless precaution: I didn't understand a word of German. Nor Portuguese, the language Nuno used to communicate.

"In an hour the Frau will be at a fashion house on Prinz Eugen-Straße, where there's a nice sitting room with coffee and cookies."

"I'll be there."

After confirming the appointment, the man put away his phone and looked at me. "I was sure you'd accept. You never know when to give up."

"You said it yourself," I scoffed, "you're a real connoisseur of the human spirit."

"And that's precisely why I suggest you listen to Frau Vieira. She's a very understanding woman."

He turned heel and headed to his car. As he pulled away he

made a lighthearted wave that I didn't know how to read. But I wasn't going to waste time thinking about it. I called Rossini and broke the news to him.

"I don't get why the madam is being so accommodating," he remarked, puzzled. "I'd have expected her to send two gonzos to knock the tar out of you."

"Lucky for me she didn't," I remarked, relieved. "I think it's time we lay our cards on the table."

"But she's holding the trump card: Edith."

"Any advice?"

"Treat her the way she deserves."

The showroom belonged to an Italian stylist, an image consultant in high demand, or so I gleaned from the salesperson from Friuli while waiting for Frau Vieira to turn up. The madam was an excellent customer but never on time.

Twenty minutes later I watched a seventy-year-old matron step out of a taxi. I had no doubt it was her. She gave the impression of being the matron of a powerful family of businesspeople, with a horde of children and grandchildren, rather than the head of a criminal organization that exploited prostitutes.

I walked over to her, and she took me by the arm. "Thanks for waiting. An old lady like me isn't as agile as she once was," she said in English.

She told the attentive salespeople that she'd be using the sitting room to talk with "this handsome Italian man" and not to worry about serving us coffee, that we'd help ourselves.

"You don't do your shopping here," I said, noting the difference of style between what she had on and the fashion line of the maison.

"I pick out the patterns for my girls. The high-end girls, I mean."

She must have been an attractive woman once upon a time.

You could still make out traces of her former beauty in her lightly touched up face. Only her lipstick was conspicuous, maybe to make her lips stand out. They must have driven many men crazy once.

She asked me to fix a coffee while she selected the pastries and placed them on a small plate with her plump fingers. Her nails were painted burgundy.

"What kind of girl is Edith?" I asked.

"Why do you ask me questions you already know the answer to? Edith told me everything. We're very close."

"She's scared of you is all," I observed. "I hope you didn't hurt her."

She didn't answer. She stared at me while she sipped her coffee. "Is it true you want to take her from me?"

"Yes."

"May I ask why?"

"No. But I can assure you that I don't intend to rip her off," I told her. I wanted her to understand that I knew Edith's backstory.

"I have a theory, tell me if I'm wrong," she proceeded, ignoring what I'd just said. "You want to take her abroad to turn her into a drug mule."

I hadn't seen that coming. "What makes you think that?"

"You encountered my employee after meeting Abo Tscherne, and a few days later, at the same bar in the same hotel, you were seen with Paz Anaya Vega."

I couldn't mask my surprise, and she leapt at the chance to take command of the situation. "I pay well for my information, and waiters don't make much as it is. I know your friends by reputation only," she added before biting into a honey and lemon madeleine. "We have different interests in the hotels in Vienna, and we've always been careful not to step on each other's toes."

So that explained why she'd done me the courtesy of setting

up a civil meeting and her gorillas hadn't broken my arms and legs: she wanted to avoid entering into a conflict with the drug dealers, whom she believed I did business with.

"I've looked after Edith for many years," she continued. "I want to know what you want with her, because the fairytale she told me doesn't bear scrutiny."

"It's none of your business," I barked. "Let her go. You've already abused her enough."

"Edith is my old whore. She still turns a nice profit. If you'd like, I'll let you have her, for a fee."

"I don't buy human beings."

"Well then, I don't see how we can resolve this situation."

"There's just one way: let her go."

"And if I don't?"

I was careful not to respond. Frau Vieira was an old fox; she wanted me to threaten her to determine if I was bluffing.

She nibbled on another cookie while she waited. "I take it you won't abandon your decision to rob me of my source of income."

My silence confirmed her suspicion. Frau Vieira couldn't begin to guess the reasons for my obstinacy, and it confused her.

"I requested this meeting to find a solution," she insisted, "but at the moment I seem to be the only party interested in one."

I decided to speak her language. The only one she understood. "You're overlooking a fundamental aspect of this business: the costs and benefits. Right now all you should be asking yourself is if it's worth it to continue forcing a woman to prostitute herself rather than give her back her freedom and dignity."

"Sounds like a threat."

"Frau Vieira, you're an old madam," I explained with a pinch of contempt, "you're perfectly aware of the meaning of that word and you know it doesn't apply."

"And why's that?"

"There's no room for negotiations," I replied. "You decide. Either way, there'll be consequences."

She looked at me thoughtfully. "Maybe you're overplaying your hand. Has the thought ever occurred to you?" she said, trying not to cross the bounds of civil discourse. "This is my city. I have a good relationship with the authorities. I employ people of a certain class."

"I imagine you mean Luis Azevedo, Rui Salgueiro, and the dirty cops you pay off monthly," I shot back. "I'm familiar with your empire, Frau Vieira: solid, influential, violent, brazen. That's why I made myself crystal clear about the costs and benefits."

The madam sensed she was taking a real risk but refused to accept that sometimes it's more convenient to capitulate, quit pounding your chest, and act as if you were doing the other person a favor. Her thick-headedness would force both of us to draw this out to the bitter end.

I stood up and checked the time. "At 4 P.M. I'll pick Edith up at her place," I stated.

"Then you still have time to think it over," remarked Frau Vieira, reaching for the last cookie.

I ran back to the apartment, spooked about the consequences of my meeting.

My friends felt the same way. "We go for broke," Old Rossini kept repeating, "and see how this all shakes out."

All three of us were convinced Frau Vieira wouldn't free Edith. We were wrong. When we arrived at Edith's I saw Nuno pull up in his car and help her out. She was pressing a napkin to her cheek and seemed unsteady on her feet. The pimp dropped her on the curb and hightailed it out of there. I ran to her. She was pale, clearly in a state of shock. I saw the blood running down her neck.

"Look at what they've done," she mumbled.

They'd disfigured her. Frau Vieira had rendered her inoperable in the sex trade. She'd wanted to brand her so that Edith would always be hers.

I heard Beniamino talking on his cellphone to Martinenghi. "I need the best plastic surgeon in the city. Immediately."

A little before midnight, while Edith was resting after surgery at a high-end clinic, Rossini and I entered Leiria's. Our faces covered in scarves, we walked briskly toward the "office" of Rui Salgueiro.

He was with another guy. Unfortunately, it wasn't Nuno.

"Call Frau Vieira," I barked in English.

"What do you want me to say?" asked Rui, not taking his eye off the gun.

"Costs and benefits."

"What's that supposed to mean? Get out of here, I don't have time for this bullshit."

Beniamino put two bullets in his man, and the pimp quickly obeyed the order. After that, the Old Gangster emptied a whole magazine into Rui.

In the hallway we bumped into the woman who ran the joint. She shrugged her shoulders. Didn't say or do anything else. Maybe she'd always known, or hoped, that that was how things would end.

Max was waiting for us in the Superb, the motor running. A half hour later we were safe, for one last night, in the house on Oswaldgasse.

TEN

One late afternoon in May I was seated at a table at the Libarium in Cagliari. I was drinking an Alligator. Seven parts Calvados, three parts Drambuie, plenty of crushed ice, and a slice of green apple to nibble on when you're done, to console yourself that the glass is empty. The recipe was concocted by the creative genius Danilo Argiolas, owner of the joint.

Edith, at my side, sipped Pastis. When she sensed she was being looked at, she covered her scar with her right index finger. That bastard Nuno had used a serrated blade to keep the scar tissue from fully healing. The surgeon did what he could, over time it would fade, but she needn't get her hopes up.

It didn't bother me. I was growing increasingly fond of Edith. We'd just begun to sleep together, and I was hopelessly in love with the most beautiful and bewitching woman in the world.

Whenever I told her so, she'd burst out laughing. The word "love" had yet to escape her lips, and I wasn't really holding my breath.

I'd watch her dance and feel moved. She'd raise the volume and Natalie Merchant's voice would fill the little living room of the house we'd rented. Edith would lift her dress above her thighs and take her first steps toward a new life. We were happy together, traveled, lived from one day to the next, made do with the money that Beniamino provided us.

The Old Gangster called often for news of Edith. He never

asked about me. He knew I was happy to watch her coming
back to life, and that by concentrating on her, I could put off
having to reckon with myself.

Max wasn't in touch as often. He wrote me a long email to
say that he had returned to Padua. He had decided to
"momentarily" leave the mountain and the woman he loved in
order to throw his weight behind a party in the local election.
He used words like hope, change, turning point. Despite grueling disappointments and the price that he'd paid in the past,
the Fat Man continued to believe that politics could still play a
positive role in the country. And give meaning to his life.

"I want to stay here all summer," said Edith out of the blue.

"Seems like an excellent idea to me."

"Last night I dreamed about going back to Portugal."

"We could cross Sardinia, Corsica, France, and Spain to get
there."

"There's no rush."

She took my hand and squeezed it hard. It was her way of
letting me know that once she felt better she might go it alone.
And that she'd be sorry to see me suffer, but there was nothing
she could do about it.

My outlaw heart knew it all along. Every day was a gift, and
I'd get over another goodbye. There was an old blues song by
James Carr that summed up my situation:

At the dark end of the street
That's where we always meet
Hiding in shadows where we don't belong
Living in darkness to hide our wrong . . .

I need morphine. Or some other fucking painkiller. The wound's healing but still hurts. I feel like I've got coal in my guts. That bungling surgeon—an alcoholic, clearly, who'd been banned from practicing—couldn't manage to extract the bullet. And he had the nerve to keep complaining: "I don't have the right equipment, the patient should be admitted to a hospital immediately."

But that's not what Abo wanted. "Do what you can. It's not the end of the world if he dies."

But he did want to see me among the living, so that he could hand me over to Sabine, his bat-shit daughter with her Viking braids. I'd made her a widow when I shot her husband Guntmar.

Now I'm a guest in her basement. She comes to see me two, three times a day to check to see how I'm convalescing and whether I'll be able to handle what she has in store for me. Paz was a schoolgirl in comparison. This one's head is crammed with bunk. She goes on and on about the god Odin, his spear Gungnir, his eight-legged steed Sleipnir. And about how her children weep, how they have to grow up without a father. She says she wants to nail me to a table and rip my heart from my chest. She bought a replica of a sacrificial dagger on some basket case website. She says she's going to plant it in the exact same spot where the bullet pierced me and slice upward from there.

Did it not run counter to my interests, I'd have pointed out that the dagger didn't look sharp enough for a chisel job. I should be worried and seriously reflecting on the fact that I can't spend my entire life prisoner to pissed off women who want to carve me up. Yet every day I'm increasingly convinced that I'll walk out of this shithole on my own two legs. That's what I spend hours thinking about. About Sabine the Viking.

The poor girl's alone. She needs a man. Not only to beat her and show her a good time, like she was Odin's mother, the giantess Bestla, but to prop up her mythological drivel. And I think I can do that for her. True, I shot the man she married, but as far as I can tell, I'm the one male she's seen lately. The others seem to be avoiding her. To be honest, I'd do the same if I were them.

Had she wanted to butcher me, she'd have done so already, but I think she's been taken aback by my "courage." She's in no position to see that it's something else entirely and, for the moment, that's a good thing. Now I'm doing all I can to appear indifferent to pain and the prospect of being killed.

Yesterday I tried another angle: Guntmar died a warrior's death. I'm sure tonight she'll want to explore that thought further. I don't know shit about her Valhalla tirades, but it strikes me as logical and natural that the widow of a hero should marry another brave man.

Sabine isn't easy, she holds a grudge against me, and I still don't have a clue what she'll do. But I'm Giorgio Pellegrini. Nowhere is it written that I should die by the hand of a psychopath.

If she let her guard down just a tad to free one of my hands, her children would become good little orphans.

Lucky for me I have money stowed away all over Europe, enough to vanish into thin air and recover from these shitty experiences. Then there's always kind Toska waiting for me in Munich, and Attorney Charents and Miss Bones, who aren't actually waiting for me, but merit a visit. I have an idea knocking around in my head to return to Italy with a new identity. And maybe a nip and tuck. The fact is, I miss my country and some of my old friends. Dottoressa Marino, for one. I haven't gotten over the fact that she shot me to keep me from going around bragging about her blowjobs. And I intend to shed some light on that thorny fact. And then the *tres amigos*: Burrati, the Relic, and the Fat Man.

Everyone thinks I'm dead, and there's nothing more exciting than a resurrection. That's a surprise no one sees coming.

Anyways, what's the rush? Right now, I have to convince Sabine that I'm her darling warrior.

THE ALLIGATOR'S FAVORITE WOMEN OF THE BLUES

Cee Cee James—*Blood Red Blues, Low Down Where the Snakes Crawl*
Barbara Blue—*Sell My Jewelry*
Gina Sicilia—*Sunset Avenue, It Wasn't Real*
Anni Piper—*More Guitars than Friends*
Janiva Magness—*Love Wins Again*
Ana Popovic—*Trilogy*
Rita Chiarelli—*Breakfast at Midnight*
Ina Forsman—*Ina Forsman*
Fiona Boyes—*Box & Dice, Blues in My Heart*
Deb Callahan—*Sweet Soul*
Shaun Murphy—*It Won't Stop Raining*
Meena—*Tell Me*
Zora Young—*The French Connection*
Shemekia Copeland—*Turn the Heat Up*
Ruthie Foster—*Promise of a Brand New Day, Joy Comes Back*
Debbie Davies—*Key to Love*
Melanie Mason—*Bendin' the Blues*
Robin Rogers—*Back in the Fire*
Kellie Rucker—*Ain't Hit Bottom*
Eden Brent—*Ain't Got No Troubles*
Jane Lee Hooker—*No B!*
EG Kight—*Southern Comfort*
Nicole Hart & Anni Piper—*Split Second*
Julie Rhodes—*I'd Rather Go Blind*

Jan Jams—*Limousine Blues*
Teresa James—*The Whole Enchilada*
Joanna Connor—*Slidetime*
Deborah Coleman—*Soft Place to Fall*
Sue Foley—*Love Comin' Down*
Layla Zoe—*The Lily*
Kelley Hunt—*New Shade of Blue*
Shannon Curfman—*What You're Gettin' Into*
Lisa Mann—*Chop Water*
Mary Gauthier—*Mercy Now*
Allison Moorer—*Down to Believing*

ABOUT THE AUTHOR

Massimo Carlotto was born in Padua, Italy. In addition to the many titles in his extremely popular "Alligator" series, he is also the author of *The Fugitive*, *Death's Dark Abyss*, *Poisonville*, *Bandit Love*, and *At the End of a Dull Day*. He is one of Italy's most popular authors and a major exponent of the Mediterranean Noir novel.